Cowboy Temptation
Colt and Cassy

Cowboy Temptation Series

By
C. Deanne Rowe

Cowboy Temptation – Colt and Cassy
  Cowboy Temptation Series
by C. Deanne Rowe

Published by CDRW, L.L.C.
          Des Moines, IA

Copyright © June 2012
by C. Deanne Rowe

This book is a work of fiction. Names, places, characters, and incidents are either the product of the author's imagination, or, if real, used fictitiously. Any resemblance to actual events, locales or persons living or dead is entirely coincidental.

All Rights Reserved. Except for use in any review, the reproduction or utilization of this book is whole or in part in any form, electronic, mechanical or other means, now known or hereafter invented, including photocopying and recording, or in any information storage or retrieval system, is forbidden without the written permission of the author.

First printing June 2012

ISBN-13: 978-1467941198
ISBN-10: 1467941190

Printed in the United States of America

DEDICATION

This book is dedicated to the people in my life who have given me support, love and understanding during the time I have been pursuing my dream of writing. My first book alone is one of the biggest dreams I have had. To see this dream come true means more to me than I can express in words.

Thank you, Magnolia "Maggie" Rivers for being a teacher, writing buddy and friend.

Thanks to my Saturday Writers group and my friends at Two Rivers Romance Authors for supporting me along the way.

Thank you to Dee who took the time to read my book and give me feedback.

Most of all, thanks to my family for giving me time and space and nothing but undying support. I love you all.

Last of all I would like to say thank you to Jimmy Thomas for taking the perfect picture to grace the cover of my book. To everyone else, if you can get past the fantastic cover...Enjoy!

1

"Cowboy butts drive me nuts" Cassy read off the license plate frame. "Where in the world?"

"Laura found it. Don't you love it?" Nancy smiled.

"I do love it." Cassy held it up for inspection. "What am I supposed to do with this?"

"It goes on the back of the truck you'll be driving around the farm." Laura laughed. "It might not hurt if you drove it around town every now and then. Who knows what you might pick up?"

"Haha, very funny you guys. I'm not moving back to Oklahoma to pick up a cowboy. Although it might be nice to meet a few good looking men in tight jeans and boots while I'm there." Cassy put the present back in the box, picked up her beer and held it up in the center of the table.

"Here's to all good looking cowboys."

"Here, here." Nancy joined Cassy holding up her beer.

"Same for me." Laura joined the two friends in a toast as all three clinked their bottles together then took a drink.

"I really hate to see you leave Cassy." Laura's smile disappeared.

"Me too. It's just not the same around the office without you."

Cassy watched the expression on Nancy's face turn solemn.

"I'm going to miss you guys too but fate has played its cards for me and it's Oklahoma here I come." Cassy paused for a moment. "I wasn't sure what to do when Grandfather got sick but now I'm no longer employed by McGregor Oil, it's a good time for me to spend some time with him on the family farm."

"I can't believe you want to be a farmer," Nancy admitted. "It doesn't fit for me."

"Why? I was practically raised on the family farm and loved it. My Father, on the other hand, couldn't leave fast enough. Since he died five years ago and Grandfather is in no shape that leaves me if we want to keep the family farm up and running." Cassy explained.

"I know but I can't see you in jeans, cowboy boots and hat riding a horse along the fence to make sure the cattle can't get out or driving the Caterpillar plowing or planting the fields." Laura smiled.

"I guess you will have to visit then, both of you. There's plenty of room and I'll take you for a ride in the truck. We'll see what kind of cowboys this license plate holder attracts."

"It's a deal." Cassy laughed as both Laura and Nancy nodded their heads in agreement.

<u>2</u>

    Cassy let herself in with the spare key. The house seemed empty as she made her way to the guest bedroom.
    "Grandfather, I'm here."
    She laid her luggage down on the bed and wiped the beads of sweat from her forehead. The room looked no different than when she stayed with her grandparents over summer vacations. It must be ninety degrees outside already and yet the windows were wide open. There was nice breeze blowing through each one but it definitely wasn't cool.
    "Grandfather is still trying to save on the power bill." Cassy remembered how he would tell her that was the reason the windows were open instead of the air conditioning on. She knew her grandparents never liked to be shut up in the house. They wanted to feel part of nature and that meant outside air.
    "I guess I'm going to have to adjust."
    She opened her suitcase and pulled out a pair of shorts and a light weight blouse to change into.

Heading to the bathroom, Cassy ran cold water over her face and pulled her long brown hair up in a clip. "Much better."

"Cassandra Conner. Come give your old Grandfather a hug."

Cassy walked back into the bedroom and coming through the doorway in his wheelchair was her grandfather, James Conner.

"Grandfather." Cassy headed toward him to give him a big hug. "I was just coming to your room to find you. You look really good, up, moving around and you have lots of color in your cheeks."

"I'm having a good day so I thought I would take advantage of it. Come with me to the kitchen and let's get a cold drink. I want to catch up and hear all about your trip."

"That sounds wonderful." Cassy took the handles of his wheelchair and pushed in the direction of the kitchen. "So what would you like? Some iced tea, some juice or maybe some milk and cookies."

"I vote for milk and cookies. Those darn nurses try to keep me on a diet because of this stupid diabetes."

"Well, then milk and cookies it will be. I'm sure there's something in here we can snack on." Cassy searched through the sparsely filled pantry and found a stash of sugar free cookies. She poured each of them a glass of milk and put a few cookies on a plate and carried them to the table.

"Here we go. Enjoy."

"So tell me about your trip Cassandra."

Cassy watched as her grandfather took a bite of cookie and a drink of milk.

"Not much to tell Grandfather. It was long and tiring. I left early so I wouldn't be driving very long in this heat."

"You made good time. It's still early in the day. Well, I'm glad you're here. I've really missed seeing you."

"I'm sorry I haven't visited more often but, work was crazy this past year. It seemed there was always some project to do. That was when I was under the impression I was a valued employee of the company and killing myself with work was actually going to get me ahead." Cassy paused for a minute. "I guess they proved me wrong."

"There's one thing I want you to promise me Cassandra."

She could see the concern on his face as he reached for her hand.

"What's that?"

"I know you're coming back to help because of my health, but I don't want you to make this farm your first priority. There's so much more out there for you. You're a young woman and you have your entire life ahead of you. Your grandmother lived and breathed this farm and it killed her."

He paused for a moment as Cassy noticed the creases in his face deepen.

"Well, this farm and me. We worked her to death. It's a hard life Cassandra."

"I know Grandfather, but you know what, Grandmother wouldn't have had any other life. She loved you and this farm. This was where she wanted to be and she was happy. She always told me her life was complete. But if it will make you happy, I promise you I'll let you know if the farm gets to be too much. I'm not having my stuff moved out here until I'm sure I'm staying. How about that?" Cassy patted his hand.

"Sounds good to me. I'll hold you to it. Cassandra, you're a bright young lady. There will always be something out there for you to do. There will be other career paths for you to prove you're a valuable asset. Heck, I've known that since you were a little girl."

"You have to think that because you love me Grandfather. I'm your granddaughter. But thanks for trying to make me feel better. Let's change the subject. So now, you tell me what's going on with the farm. What am I getting myself into?"

Cassy picked up the empty plate and retrieved the milk from the refrigerator. She poured them some more milk and placed a few more cookies on the plate.

"Well, we added a few more head of cattle, started charging for stud fees and selling semen from our prize bulls, planted a few more acres of wheat and soy beans. I believe we actually turned a profit this year."

Cassy noticed her grandfather's shoulder pull back with pride.

"So how is your help working out? You must have some good people and they must be doing all right for you to show a profit."

"I only have one farmhand. When we're done here we'll go out and meet Colt. He's the reason the farm is doing so well. He's a hard worker. I think you two will get along great."

"Let me clean up here then we'll go." Cassy picked up the plate and glasses, rinsed them off in the sink.

"Okay, let's go." Cassy started wheeling her grandfather towards the door when a muscular, tan, and tight jeaned cowboy walked straight out of her dreams and through the kitchen door. He took off his cowboy hat and ran his hands through his thick coal black hair. Cassy couldn't take her gaze off him.

"Mr. Conner. I hope I'm not interrupting." His voice was deep and almost as sexy as he was.

"Not at all Colt. Come on in. We were just headed out to meet you." James motioned for Colt to come closer.

"You were?"

"Cassandra, this is Colt Matthews. I was just telling you about him. Colt, this is my Granddaughter, Cassandra Conner."

Cassy watched closely as he walked towards her. She wished she had taken more time picking out something to wear now and maybe freshened up her makeup instead of just running cold water over her face. Had she known she was going to be meeting someone as handsome as Colt Matthews, she would have.

"It's nice to meet you, Ms. Conner." Colt extended his hand.

Cassy shook his hand noticing how hers seemed to disappear. His grip was firm and his palm slightly calloused.

"Please, Colt, call me Cassy."

"Cassy. That's a nice name."

A smile came across his face which seemed to light up his entire expression. He had one corner which turned up a little crooked giving him that bad boy look. Cassy was sure when he was young his Mother had no problem telling what he was up to.

"Thanks." She could feel her skin begin to blush. It was like she was back in high school.

"I just came in to tell you, Mr. Conner, I finished repairing the fence on the North end."

Colt may have taken his eyes off Cassy but hers were firmly fixed on him.

"Good job. If you hadn't noticed the break in the fencing, we might have lost some of the cattle." James reached to shake his hand.

"I took a head count and everybody is accounted for. I'm going to go into town and get some supplies and grab some lunch. Did you make your list?" Colt asked.

"Yes, I did. It's over there on the counter. Let me get you some money." Cassy watched her grandfather grab the wheels of his chair and began to turn.

"I'll get it Grandfather. Tell me where you keep your money and I'll be right back."

"No, I'll grab it. You stay here and keep Colt company."

Cassy watched her grandfather wheel himself into the next room leaving her alone with Colt in a complete silence.

"Can I get you something to drink? It's very hot outside." Cassy fanned herself with her hand and tried to act like she wasn't uncomfortable. She was positive it wasn't the weather making her hot. There was something about Colt which pulled her to him. Cassy had always had people radar, her father called it. Her radar was going off all over the place while he was in the room. The problem was she wasn't sure if it was good or bad.

"How about a glass of cold water?' Colt took a seat at the kitchen table.

"Sure." She took the pitcher of cold water out of the refrigerator and poured him a glass, watching as he took a sip. His skin was nice and tan with a little speckle of whiskers. He wasn't bad looking and he was a real Oklahoma cowboy.

"So what brought you back to your grandpa's farm Cassy?"

"I was laid off from my job in the City. I thought I would take a little time and see if I could help Grandfather since he's alone."

"Sorry to hear about your job. I'm sure your grandpa loves having you here to visit though."

Cassy took a seat at the table as she watched Colt take another sip of his water.

"I'm also sure he told you the farm was running smoothly. He wouldn't need your help here."

"Losing my job wasn't easy to accept at first but I'm getting used to it. I'm sure you're doing a great job on the farm, Colt. I'm not here to take your job." Cassy could feel herself becoming frustrated. Didn't he know if something happened to her grandfather, she would be his boss? She was beginning to feel she was right back at McGregor Oil fighting for her position in a male dominated environment. The last thing she wanted to do right after arriving was revive those feelings.

"I could tell when I drove up everything looks great. But being here also gives me time to spend with Grandfather before...well, you know." Cassy picked at the piece of lint on the tablecloth.

"Your grandpa is a tough old bird. He's going to give death a run for its money. You wait and see." There it was again. That smile sent chills down her spine.

Cassy suddenly felt the warmth of Colt's hand on top of hers comforting her. She jerked her hand back before she realized what she had done.

What am I so afraid of?

"Here you go Colt. I think there's enough here to cover what I have on the list. Cassy, I didn't even think to ask if you want Colt to pick you up anything at the store while he is in town." James wheeled his chair close to the table.

"Why don't you go into town with me Cassy?" Colt stood up from the table, picked up his cowboy hat and ran his fingers through his hair.

Cassy could feel the room start heating up, or was it just her.

"That way you can pick up what you need and we'll have a chance to get to know each other."

"That's a wonderful idea Colt. It's time for me to rest anyway. You don't want to be stuck around the house with nothing to do. Let Colt show you around town." James patted Cassy's shoulder in approval.

"I've been to town lots of times Grandfather. I was going to do some unpacking and then start getting something ready for dinner." Cassy tried to come up with a legitimate excuse to get out of going with Colt. She certainly didn't like his comment about not being needed on the farm, but in a strange way she was overwhelmed by the way he was making her feel.

"Oh, go on. You'll have more fun going into town with Colt."

Before James moved his wheelchair back a little, he placed his tote containing his blood tester, test strips and insulin on his lap.

"But before you go Cassandra, will you help me into the bedroom?"

"I'll be happy to." Cassy pushed her grandfather into his bedroom and sat down on the bed. "Will you be all right while I'm gone?"

"I'll be fine. I've had to learn to like being alone since your grandma passed. You go and have a good time. I'll see you when you get back."

"Okay then." Cassy helped her grandfather into bed placing his tote on the nightstand next to his bed. "I'll go into town with Colt. I won't be long. You have a nice rest and I'll check in on you when I return. We'll have a nice dinner. I love you Grandfather." She kissed him on the forehead.

"I love you too, Cassandra. I'm really glad you are here."

Cassy watched as he made himself comfortable on the bed and then start taking everything necessary to test his blood from his tote. She placed a blanket next to him on the bed in case he wanted a cover.

"You know Cassandra, Colt is right. Your name is beautiful and so are you."

"Thank you, Grandfather. Have a nice rest."

Cassy stopped in her bedroom to freshen her makeup. She grabbed her purse from her bed and walked back into the kitchen.

"I'm ready."

"Great. Let's go."

Colt waved his cowboy hat and motioned for Cassy to go ahead of him, staying in step close behind her placing his hat on his head. She walked out the backdoor as Colt held it open. As she past she noticed his musky scent and felt the heat from his body close to hers.

"My truck is right over here."

Cassy watched Colt sprint ahead of her and open the passenger door, holding her arm as she climbed inside. She settled in the seat and waited as he slid in behind the wheel. Cassy couldn't help but laugh. She would have never believed it if someone had told her a week ago she would be in Oklahoma in the truck of an Adonis named Colt Matthews, heading into town for supplies. Her world had definitely turned full circle.

3

"That should be it. Are you ready to head back?" Colt pushed the cart towards the register.

"I think we got everything on the list." Cassy took one last look over the list her grandfather made.

"Why don't you go ahead? You have a lot less than I do." Colt held the basket so Cassy could go walk ahead of him to the register. "What is all that stuff?"

"Just some make up, moisturizer, shampoo and conditioner. Why?" Cassy asked.

"You don't need all that stuff."

Colt smiled at Cassy sending another shock through her body. She wished she knew how long it was going to take her to get used to that smile.

"Thank you." Cassy, still feeling the effects of his last smile, wasn't quite sure how to answer. "I don't know if I believe you though. All women need a little help."

"It's your money to waste. But if you ask me, you would be beautiful with or without all that junk."

Cassy tried not to let drool fall from the corners of her mouth as she watched Colt lean over the handle of the cart balancing himself with his brawny arms. The muscles of his chest pressed against the material of his t-shirt making them more than noticeable. She placed her small basket up on the register trying her best not to let Colt know what pleasure his body and last comment gave her.

"Thank you." Making an effort to change the topic of conversation, Cassy asked, "So, Colt, besides working on the farm what else do you like to do? Do you have any hobbies?"

"I ride bulls at rodeos. I'm actually the title holder for the state rodeo." Cassy didn't have a hard time imagining him in his tight jeans, chaps and cowboy hat twisting and turning on top of a bucking bull. In fact, the thought excited her. She was finding herself jealous of the bull.

"Really. That's impressive. Maybe you'll ride sometime soon and Grandfather and I can come and watch."

"I do have a rodeo coming up in the next month not far away. You're welcome to come."

"Let me know when it is and I'll see what Grandfaher's got planned." Cassy handed money to the cashier and waited for her change.

"You know looking at all this food is making me hungry. How about if we stop at the City Café down the street and grab a bite before we go back to the farm?" Colt asked.

"I'm actually hungry myself. That sounds good. I bet you don't get to eat out very often since you live on the farm."

"Not often. I take every opportunity I get." Colt watched as the cashier scanned his items and bagged them. Cassy watched Colt.

"I need a couple bags of ice, too." He handed her money, took his change and began pushing the cart out the door of the store to his truck.

"Why the ice?" Cassy followed close behind.

"We need to keep some of this stuff cold. I have a cooler in the back of the truck."

"You think of everything." Cassy told Colt. "So what do they have that's good at the café?"

"They have a great burger, if you like burgers. They always have the daily special which is guaranteed to put a few pounds on you. It's normally something fried with a biscuit and gravy. Whatever you order, you'll like."

Cassy watched Colt load the bags in the back of his truck. She liked the way his flexing muscles shimmered from the sun and sweat. He was a nice looking man but there still was something Cassy wasn't sure about. She was going to have to get past it because they were going to have to work together. If she was going to make a go of running the family farm, she was going to have to trust Colt to get her up to speed.

"I gotta grab the ice. Why don't you load the rest in the cooler?"

Cassy climbed in the back of Colt's truck, opened the lid of the cooler and started loading the dairy items from the bags. Colt came back with two bags of ice and placed them carefully on top of the items then shut the lid and picked up a tarp lying in the back and threw it across the top.

"That should keep them cold until we get back to the farm. Are you ready to go eat?" Colt asked extending his hand to help Cassy down.

"Yes." Cassy took his hand then climbed down and into the passenger side of the truck.

****

The City Café wasn't busy at all.

"Colt Mathews, what can I get for you?" A female voice came from behind Cassy as they checked out the empty booths.

"Fannie." Colt replied as they both turned to see an older lady walking up behind them.

"We stopped in for lunch. What's your special today?" Colt asked.

Fannie came to the table. "You're looking good there Colt."

"Thanks Fannie." When Colt put his massive arms around her and gave her a hug she seemed to disappear.

"Homemade chicken pot pie is the daily special." Fannie managed to get out when Colt finally released her.

"That sounds good but I think I'll stick with a cheeseburger and a coke." Cassy replied as she took a seat in the booth.

"I'll take the same but with a cold beer. By the way Fannie, this is Cassy Conner."

"Conner you say. You aren't James Conner's grandkid are you?" Fannie asked.

"Yes, I am." Cassy smiled. "You know my grandfather?"

"Yes. You forget it's a small town. I heard you were coming to town. Welcome dear. So you think you're gonna run the family farm? Didn't your grandfather teach you that's a man's job? A pretty little thing like you shouldn't concern herself which such things. Colt here is doing a wonderful job for your grandfather. I don't know why you would want that to change."

Cassy got the distinct impression Fannie was a big fan of Colt Matthews.

"No, he didn't tell me it was a man's job and I didn't say anything was going to change."

"Well then maybe after you've been here a few weeks you'll find out its hard work running a farm. I'm sure it's not quite the job you had in the big City, but then you lost that didn't you?" Fannie shot Cassy a slight grin. "If you decide you want a woman's job, I can always use some help around the café."

Cassy looked at Colt for some help with the conversation. He shrugged his shoulders and smiled that crooked little smile.

"I'll keep that in mind Fannie." Cassy wasn't sure exactly where Fannie's attitude towards her was coming from. After all, she had just met the woman. She decided to let it pass this time. Next time she would be more on the defensive.

"Sure deary. You just let me know."

Cassy laughed as Fannie disappeared behind the counter to pour a beer.

"Thanks for all the help there Colt." Cassy snapped. "Fannie is one strong willed, opinionated woman who I believe likes you a lot. She's also under the impression I'm coming here to take your job from you. I wonder where she would get an idea like that."

Cassy noticed a slight grin beginning on Colt's face as he rubbed his fingers across his lips to try and hide it.

"I come in here as much as I can. Fannie is easy to talk to. In fact, I thought about fixin' your grandfather up with Fannie. I think they would hit it off don't you?"

"Don't do me any favors, please." Cassy requested. "She already doesn't like me. If I didn't know better, I would think she is trying to protect you from me." Cassy could feel her pulse quicken and a shock run through her body as Colt took her hands in his then moved closer. This time she was not going to give him the satisfaction of knowing he made her uncomfortable by pulling her hand away. After all she was enjoying the view as he moved a little closer. He had the most beautiful deep dark brown eyes and a solid chin to support the striking features of his face. He still had a little stubble on his cheeks which Cassy liked.

"You're going to need a strong, capable man to protect a pretty little thing like you. Are you sure you want me to leave you at the mercy of Fannie?"

Cassy couldn't stop looking into his eyes and she certainly couldn't say anything.

Colt finally let go of her hand as Fannie returned placing their drinks on the table in front of them.

"Aren't you two cozy? Your burgers will be out in a few. Is there anything else you two need?"

"We're fine Fannie. Thanks."

Colt smiled at Cassy. As if his touch didn't send her over the edge, there was that smile again.

The rest of lunch was eaten in almost complete silence. Cassy knew Colt realized he had gotten to her mentally and excited her physically. The last thing she needed was him to know he could make her weak.

****

"It was nice to meet you Fannie."

Colt noticed Cassy gave him an 'I'm trying to be nice' stare as she headed for the door.

"I'll wait for you outside Colt."

"I'll be out as soon as I settle up here with Fannie." Colt watched Cassy walk out the front door admiring the perfect shape of her legs. The thought of them wrapped around him excited him.

"So what do I owe you?"

"I'm over here."

Fannie chuckled as Colt felt his face turn red. He had been caught but it was worth it.

"You know what they say about fishin' off the company dock?" Fannie remarked. "Here's your total." She handed a ticket to Colt. "I know you probably want a receipt since you're covering the bill for the Boss' granddaughter. I'm sure you can write it off on your taxes."

"That's why I love you Fannie. You're always taking care of me." Colt smiled.

"Remember that, would you, especially when I tell you to be careful around this one. Cassy seems like one you don't want to mess with."

"Who says I want anything to do with her? She's the Granddaughter of my boss. I'd be stupid to try anything." Colt's thoughts returned to her legs and her mouth, hot and moist, pressed up against his.

"I know you Colt Matthews. You like a challenge." Fannie laughed.

"You do know me Fannie, probably too well." Colt handed Fannie a twenty. "Keep the change."

"Thanks hun. You have a good day. Don't let it be so long before we see you again."

"I'll try Fannie. It's always a pleasure." Colt gave Fannie a wink, put on his cowboy hat and headed out the front door of the café to meet Cassy standing by the truck.

"Are you ready to head back to the farm?" Colt unlocked the truck door and opened it for Cassy. He watched as she climbed in the passenger side. Her shorts moving up her silky legs as she sat down in the truck seat. Shutting the door, Colt couldn't help but notice the outline of her breast as she clipped the seatbelt around her.

"Not bad." He whispered shaking his head as he walked around the truck to the driver's side.

"Is everything all right?" Cassy asked as Colt opened his door.

"Yeah, why?" Colt climbed into the truck and shut the door.

"I thought I heard you say something."

"Sorry. I didn't say a thing." Colt smiled. "Let's head back." He started the truck and backed out of the parking spot. "Did you enjoy lunch?"

"It was good. Thank you, by the way, for buying. Next time it's my turn."

"So there's going to be a next time?" Colt liked that thought. "It's a date."

"I don't think you can call it a date." Cassy exclaimed. "I'm sure there will be plenty of times we can come into town together to get supplies."

"Of course. We wouldn't want anyone in town to know we were dating." Colt could tell by the look on Cassy's face he was frustrating her. There was nothing he enjoyed more than to know he was making someone uncomfortable, especially a beautiful woman.

"Stop it Colt. You know what I mean."

"I'm just teasing you Cassy. Don't take everything I say so seriously."

"Fine."

Colt watched out of the corner of his eye as Cassy adjusted herself in the seat. He had gotten to her and it made him happy. He could feel the excitement rushing through his body. He was going to have to learn her limit so he would know how far to push her comfort level. Fannie was right, he enjoyed a challenge.

4

Cassy picked up a few packages from the back of the truck and carried them into the kitchen. The house was dark and quiet. She realized they had been gone longer than they planned. Cassy thought for sure her grandfather would be awake by now. There were no dishes in the sink from lunch. Heading towards the bedroom, she wanted to make sure he was awake. It would be time for dinner in a few hours.

"Grandfather, how are you doing?" Cassy asked as she sat down on the edge of the bed. Her grandfather didn't respond. She could hear his breathing was shallow. Taking his hand in hers, she could feel he was clammy. Cassy noticed he was sweating even though he wasn't covered. "Something's not right. Colt." She ran to the kitchen. "Colt, help me."

"What's wrong?"

"Something's wrong with Grandfather. He's not waking up." She ran back to the bedroom with Colt right behind her.

"Let me check." She watched as he felt his neck for a pulse. "His pulse is faint. Call 911."

Cassy picked up the phone next to her grandfather's bed and dialed. She gave them the address and information.

"Tell them he's diabetic and his blood sugars extremely low. Tell them to hurry."

Cassy repeated what Colt had told her. "Yes, thank you. I won't hang up."

"He's past the point of eating or drinking juice to bring up his sugars."

Cassy watched Colt grab her grandfather's tote. He took out the monitor, a test strip and what looked like an ink pen. He lifted up her grandfather's hand and pushed the pen against the tip of his finger and placed a drop of blood on the test strip. Slipping the strip into the monitor he watched the numbers register on the display. He opened the drawer of the nightstand next to the bed. He pulled out a red box. She remembered seeing her grandmother do the same thing before. He took a pen out of the case and gave her grandfather a shot.

"What did you give him?"

"I gave him a glucose shot to help bring up his blood sugar levels. It takes a few minutes to start working. Hopefully by the time the ambulance arrives."

Those few minutes seemed like an eternity. Cassy put the phone down on the nightstand ran to the kitchen door after hearing the sirens coming up the road. Watching them grab their medical bags from the ambulance, she opened the door to show them the way. One of the paramedics ran in front of her making his way directly to her grandfather's bedroom.

"How's he doing Colt?"

"Lucas. He's still out of it." Colt moved away from the bed to the doorway so Lucas could sit down. "I gave him a glucose shot just a few minutes ago."

"That should help," Lucas turned towards Cassy. "Who are you?"

"I'm his granddaughter."

"So you're Mr. Conner's granddaughter? What's your name Granddaughter?"

"Cassy. My name is Cassy."

"It's nice to meet you Cassy, I'm Lucas. Lucas Harding. I'd shake your hand but I'm a little occupied." He looked up at her and for the first time since he arrived and she caught a glimpse of one of the most gorgeous men she had seen in a long time. Well, at least since she met Colt Matthews. His eyes were robin's egg blue and his dark, thick eyelashes framed his oval eyes perfectly. She watched as he took her grandfather's blood pressure and checked his pulse. After a few minutes he checked his blood sugar levels.

"Mr. Conner. It's Lucas. You remember me don't you? Mr. Conner." Lucas turned to Cassy. "Did he eat anything today?"

"We had some milk and cookies this morning after I arrived. I made sure they were sugar free. That's all I know he has eaten since I got here." Cassy looked for Colt to see if he agreed but he was gone.

"It sure looks like he took a little too much insulin. He's unresponsive and sweating profusely. He'll be all right in a few minutes."

Lucas stayed right with him until he began to come around. The other paramedic checked him every few minutes to make sure his body was responding properly. Cassy watched carefully trying to see if she could tell what they were doing.

After half an hour her grandfather seemed to be coming around. Lucas went into the kitchen, poured him a glass of milk and brought him a banana. He sat back down next to him on the bed.

"Here you go Mr. Conner. Drink some of this milk."

Her grandfather's hands were still shaky but he took the glass of milk and began to drink. Cassy watched as Lucas carefully peeled the skin of the banana back.

"Here, how about if I trade you." Lucas said.

He took the glass of milk and handed her grandfather the banana.

"Try eating some of this." Lucas instructed.

The other paramedic checked his blood again and nodded his head.

"It looks like you're almost back to normal Mr. Conner. That's great. Why don't you finish that banana and Cassy and I will talk for a few minutes." Lucas stood up from the bed, took Cassy by the arm and headed out the bedroom door.

"You were wonderful with him. Thank you so much."

"Do you know how to take care of his diabetes? Do you know what to feed him and how to help him count his carbohydrates?" Lucas asked.

"No, not really. I just know my grandmother wouldn't let him have sweets and he ate lots of chicken, fish and vegetables."

"How about if I bring you some reading material? I can stop by sometime when I'm off duty and go over it with you, if you like. How long are you going to be here with your grandfather?"

"I'll be here for a while. I just arrived today."

"Right now why don't you sit with your grandfather while I finish up?"

Cassy watched as Lucas walked out the door. She had never imagined such a small town would have two gorgeous hunks of men and that she would meet them both in one day. Nancy and Laura weren't going to believe her. She headed back into the bedroom and sat down on the edge of the bed by her grandfather.

"You really gave me a scare Grandfather. "

"I'm sorry. It's just sometimes I take too much insulin. I'm not really good at remembering what I've eaten or counting the carbohydrates. We ate those cookies so I took a little extra insulin. It must have been too much. Since you're here maybe you can help me keep track of my food."

"I'll be happy to. You and Lucas are going to have to teach me what to do. I'm a quick learner." Cassy smiled at him. She could tell he was still trying to regain his composure.

"I'll teach you everything I know. After that, you'll have to ask Lucas. He's very knowledgeable about medical stuff."

"I noticed. It seems like he has been here a few times. He knows you pretty well."

"Yes, he's been here a time or two. He works hard. They don't make 'em like Lucas anymore." James smiled.

"They sure don't." Cassy looked at her grandfather's shirt wet from perspiration. "Let me get you a dry shirt and then we can go into the kitchen and get you some more milk and something else to eat. I can put the supplies away while you tell me where they go."

"Sounds like a deal to me."

Cassy helped him change then get out of bed and into his wheelchair. They headed out the bedroom door to the kitchen.

"I'm glad you're here Cassandra. I thought I could do it on my own but I realize I need you right now."

Cassy reached down and hugged her grandfather. "I'm glad I'm here too. I can't think of anywhere else I would rather be."

****

Cassy started putting the groceries away as her grandfather sat at the kitchen table having a bowl of sugar free ice cream.

"Looks like you are feeling better and found something to eat." Lucas sat down at the table next to James.

"Can't beat a good bowl of ice cream, even if it's not the real stuff. You want some?" James asked.

"No thanks Mr. Conner. My partner is waiting for me. I just came back to talk to your granddaughter and then I have to get back to work. I promised Cassy I would stop by sometime and you and I would go over with her how to count your carbohydrates and how she can help you take care of your diabetes."

"That's nice of you Lucas. When do you get off work?" James asked.

"I should get off around five. That is if we don't have any calls that keep me out."

"Why don't you stop by after work and have dinner with Cassandra and me? How does some baked chicken and vegetables sound?" James asked. "Maybe a nice green salad."

"That sounds really good Mr. Conner but I don't want to impose. I can stop by sometime when it's a little more convenient."

"Nonsense. You're welcome to stop by for dinner. Right Cassandra?"

"Right Grandfather." Cassy smiled. "You're more than welcome to join us for dinner. It's no trouble at all."

"In that case, I would love to. It would be nice to have a home cooked meal." Lucas smiled.

Cassy thought she was going to melt right there into the linoleum on the floor. This time it wasn't the fact it was 90 degrees outside, it was the look in Lucas' eyes.

"I've got to get back now. I guess I'll see the two of you around five."

Cassy watched him stand up and walk towards the door.

"Make sure he behaves himself until then."

"I will." Cassy replied. "Thank you again, Lucas."

She just realized one of the most handsome men in the State of Oklahoma is coming to dinner tonight and she needed to look good plus cook. There were no restaurants to grab take out, no place to call that delivered edible cuisine, she had to cook.

"Now what am I going to do?"

<u>5</u>

    Cassy finished putting the last of the groceries away. After a day like today, she needed to soak in a nice bath before starting dinner. It had been a long day of traveling, taking a trip into town with Colt and then her grandfather having a problem with his blood sugar. A bath would be the perfect answer to help her de-stress. Colt had come back in to check on her grandfather and they were going over business at the kitchen table.
    "Since you guys are occupied I'm going to take a quick bath before I start dinner. Colt, you're coming to dinner right? Grandfather invited Lucas. You're welcome to join us."
    "Sure, why not."
    Cassy saw his eyes light up at the prospect.
    "Thanks."
    "Great. Lucas will be here around five. Why don't you come back then if you aren't still here going over business." Cassy headed towards the bathroom.
    "Don't get all dolled up for me Cassy." Colt smiled.

"Don't worry Colt. If I get dolled up, it certainly won't be for you. Fannie might get jealous."

Cassy was going to get all dolled up, but for whom, she couldn't say. She was having dinner with two gorgeous men. Who would have ever thought? She would like to think she could pick between Lucas and Colt but flipping a coin might be an option.

****

Sticking her big toe up against the faucet made the running water spray out against the side of the tub. Cassy could hear her grandmother's voice.

"Cassandra stop doing that or you are going to get your toe stuck in the faucet and we will have to cut it off."

She laid her head back on the edge of the tub. This was the first chance she had gotten to relax since she arrived. It felt good. She found her mind wandering, thinking about Lucas. He was so easy to talk to. Normally she was tongue tied and awkward around men she just met. For some reason Lucas didn't make her feel that way at all. She was at ease with him.

Then there was Colt. His touch sent sparks through her. She went straight from nothing to aching for his touch. He made her more than a little uncomfortable so her guard was up with him.

She was looking forward to seeing Lucas again tonight even if Colt was going to be there, too. She could pull this off. She could manage to have dinner with both of them and not have a problem. Hopefully Colt would behave and allow everyone to enjoy themselves.

****

Cassy took the chicken out of the refrigerator along with the lettuce and salad dressing.

"How about if you let me cook the chicken on the grill since it's so hot? We won't heat up the house and you can make the rest of the meal. Sound like a deal?" Colt asked.

"Sounds good to me. Are you sure?" Cassy asked as she put the chicken on a platter and seasoned it.

"I grill a mean chicken. Wait and see."

"I hate to make you work since we invited you over for dinner."

"It's not a problem. I love grilling. I'll go get it started and come back in to see if there is anything else I can help you with."

"It's ready when you are. I'll start the vegetables and set the table." Cassy handed Colt the platter of chicken.

"It's going to be nice to have a woman around the house again isn't it Mr. Conner?" Lucas commented as he walked in the kitchen door. "I hope I'm not late."

"You're right on time Lucas. Come on in." James replied.

"Colt was just going to put the chicken on the grill. Would you like something to drink Lucas?" Cassy asked.

"I'd love a beer, if you have one."

"There are some in refrigerator. Why don't you help yourself?" Cassy washed her hands then rinsed the head of lettuce tearing it apart.

"Can I get you a beer Colt?" Lucas asked.

"Sure. Why don't you grab one for both of us and keep me company while I grill?"

"I'll be right out."

Cassy watched as Lucas twisted the tops off two beer bottles and headed out the back door.

"Those two seem to be chummy." Cassy smiled at her grandfather. "Are they friends?"

"You forget it's a small town Cassy. Everyone knows everyone. Colt and Lucas are two single guys. They have a lot in common." James replied.

"They are completely different. I don't see what they have in common at all."

"What do you mean Cassy?"

"Well, they are both nice looking, I'll give them that. But from what I can tell, Colt is a 'man's man' and hard to predict. Lucas, on the other hand, is a nice person but seems a little distant."

"I don't know what makes you think that about Colt. He's a good guy. You just have to get to know him. I'm sure he will be different when he gets to know you. I agree with you about Lucas, though. He's nice enough but I've always thought he was reserved. Never could quite read him."

Cassy finished cutting up a tomato and cucumber from the garden. She tossed dressing through the salad and put it on the table. The green beans were simmering on the stove along with the bacon Cassy had sliced and added to them. She had also put some red potatoes in a pot of water to boil. Everything smelled wonderful but needed a little bit longer.

"Just enough time to check on the guys and see how the grilling is going." Cassy washed her hands and headed out the back door.

****

After finishing dinner, Lucas helped Cassy clear off the table and put the leftovers away. Colt sat at the table with James talking business. Cassy and Lucas sat down with her grandfather and Colt. They went over everything he had for dinner even the bowl of ice cream he had before dinner. Lucas showed Cassy how to count the carbohydrates James had eaten. He prepared a needle with the right amount of insulin and handed it to Cassy to administer the shot.

"I don't know if I can do this!" Cassy looked at the needle. She didn't remember her grandfather having to take shots until the past few years. He was always able to manage his blood sugars with diet and exercise. When her grandmother passed away was when her grandfather seemed to lose ground on his fight to keep his diabetes under control.

"You can't hurt him." Lucas explained. "It needs to go in a muscle not in a vein. A good place to give him the shot is in his thigh or in his stomach away from his navel."

Cassy watched as Lucas showed her how to mark off the area around his navel but she still couldn't bring herself to push the needle in his skin.

"Here, I'll guide you."

Lucas took her hand and stuck the needle in James' stomach then pushed as the insulin slowly flowed from the needle into his body.

"That wasn't so hard right?"

"Not really." Cassy shuddered. "I'll have to try it again to make sure."

"If you guys are through using me as a pin cushion, I'm going to go get ready for bed."

James turned his wheelchair around and headed for his bedroom. "It was nice having company for dinner. It's usually just me and Colt. I enjoyed it. We'll have to do it again."

"Good night Grandfather. I love you. I'll see you in the morning." Cassy watched her grandfather make his way to his bedroom. "I'll come in and check on you before I go to bed."

"Good night Cassandra. I love you, too. Good night Lucas. See you tomorrow Colt."

"Good night Mr. Conner. I'll be here to have breakfast with you bright and early tomorrow morning." Colt smiled at Cassy. "I guess I'm going to call it a night also. How about you Lucas?"

"I want to go over a few more things with Cassy and then I'll be leaving." Lucas stood up and shook Colt's hand. "It was good to see you again Colt."

"You too, Lucas. Thanks for your help with the chicken." Colt ran his fingers through his hair then put his cowboy hat on. "I'll see you in the morning Cassy."

"Good night." Cassy watched him disappear out the kitchen door. She was glad she was finally alone with Lucas. Now maybe she could get to know him better. Maybe she could figure out why he acted like he had something to hide.

"You're really good with Grandfather. It's nice to know he has had you around the last few years to take care of him."

"I'm kinda fond of the old man. He reminds me of my grandfather."

"Where is your family?" Cassy paused. "Do you mind me asking?"

"I only have my mother left. My grandparents died when I was a child. My father took off when I was two or so. I've never knew him."

"So is your Mother around here?"

"Sort of. She's in a nursing home. She has Alzheimer's. I try to visit as much as I can but she doesn't even know me."

Cassy noticed the expression on his face changed from the carefree Lucas to one of deep thought and hurt. That has to be why he is so reserved at times.

"I'm sorry. I can't imagine. That must be painful."

"Don't be sorry. Every now and then she'll remember and it's worth the wait."

Cassy could see in his eyes how much he loved his Mother as he talked about her condition. She could almost feel her heart melting.

"It's about time for me to leave."

As Cassy walked with Lucas to his truck, she tried to carry on a conversation. "I'm glad you could come to dinner. I enjoyed our talk."

"Me too." Lucas replied. "Thank you for everything Cassy. Maybe we can do it again sometime?"

"I would love that." Cassy smiled.

"Great. Well, I have to go. Let me give you my cell phone number so if you need anything you call me. Anything at all." Lucas pulled a card out of his wallet and handed it to Cassy.

"Thanks. I'll make sure and call if I need to."

"You can also call just because. I wouldn't mind it at all."

Even in the dark Cassy could see the sparkle in his eyes when he smiled.

"I might just do that." Cassy liked the thought of seeing him again or just talking to him on the phone. She realized it was going to get lonely here after awhile.

"I better go. Thanks again."

Cassy waited as he climbed in the pickup and drove away before she headed back to the house. Shutting the doors and locking up, she stopped and checked on her grandfather. He seemed to be sleeping peacefully. He was breathing normally and his color was good. If she didn't know better she could swear he was smiling. She bent down and kissed him lightly on the forehead. "I love you, Grandfather."

As Cassy made her way to her bedroom she held the card Lucas had given her tightly in her hand running her fingers over the raised lettering. She found a safe place for it in the top drawer of her nightstand. Slipping into her nightgown, Cassy climbed into bed. She wasn't going to have any trouble finding something or someone to dream about tonight.

****

"Hey, what's going on?" Cassy asked as she walked into the kitchen. "The sun isn't even up and you guys are in here making all kinds of noise."

"Good morning to you too sunshine." James Conner smiled. "You're going to have to get used to early hours if you are going to run this farm."

"Good morning Cassy." Colt smiled.

"Come on Grandfather, you don't have to get up before the crack of dawn to run a farm. This isn't a dairy farm. You have always been an early riser." Cassy sat down at the table and laid her head down. "I remember Grandmother saying she couldn't keep you in bed past six o'clock if she wanted to."

"You can sleep when you're dead is what I always say. Why don't you go get dressed and Colt and I will make you some breakfast."

"Sure, I'll get dressed." Cassy stood up and headed out the kitchen door. "I'll take my eggs over easy."

She headed to the bedroom and slipped on a pair of jeans and a t-shirt. Cassy sat down on the bed while she brushed her hair then pulled it back in a ponytail. She opened the drawer of the nightstand next to the bed and took out the business card Lucas gave her last night. Cassy fell asleep thinking about Lucas and how she was looking forward to seeing him again but somehow during the night her dreams turned to Colt. Why would they turn to him? She was trying her best to keep him out of her thoughts but somehow he kept working his way back in. Finishing her hair, Cassy headed back to the kitchen.

"Here you go." Colt sat a plate of eggs, bacon and toast down on the table. "Over easy just like you ordered."

"These look great. Thanks Colt." Cassy joined her grandfather at the table and started eating her breakfast. Colt brought her a glass of milk and sat it down in front of her.

"Wow, the service is better here than it was yesterday at the café." Cassy smiled at Colt. "I guess I need to leave you a tip."

"Feel free." Colt smiled. "Or you can pay me back by making dinner tonight then maybe after dinner we can go into town and go dancing. You know how to line dance don't you?"

"Dancing? I haven't been dancing in a long time." Cassy took a bite of her eggs. "That sounds like fun but I'm going to have to pass. Yesterday was a long day. I'd like to spend tonight around the house. Thank you for the invitation though."

"You two kids go into town and have a good time. Don't feel like you have to stick around the house and take care of an old man. I'll be fine."

"That's not it at all. I need to catch up on my sleep from the past few days and I'd like to have a nice quiet evening. How about if I get a rain check Colt?"

"Sure Cassy. We'll find another weekend."

Thoughts of dancing with Colt, him holding her tight against his muscular body, both of them swaying to the beat of the music began running through Cassy's head sending desire for him flowing. She was totally confused about what she was feeling for Colt and Lucas. Lucas was sweet and gorgeous. Then there was Colt, strong, manly, and ruggedly handsome and sexy as hell.

Going dancing with Colt sometime would give her a chance to get to know him better. She was a little nervous about the possibility but strangely looking forward to it. Maybe they would run into Lucas. After all it was a small town. What else do people around her have to do on a Saturday night?

6

    Cassy cleaned up the kitchen after Colt and her grandfather had been kind enough to make her breakfast. When she finished, she decided to take a trip around the farm. She wanted to see all the changes Colt had made.
    "Grandfather, do you want to go for a ride? I want to check out the farm." Cassy asked as she grabbed a hat from the mud room, slipped her cell phone in her pocket and picked up the truck keys. She walked into the living room. "How about it? I need a tour guide."
    "Sure. It's been awhile since I've been out in the fields. Let's go take a look."
    Cassy rolled his wheelchair into the kitchen and handed him his cane.
    "It's going to be a hot one today. We won't be gone very long." Cassy helped her grandfather walk out to the truck and climb in then she climbed in the driver's side.
    "This reminds me of old times. You would always take me with you when you went out to inspect the fences or check the crops."

"You loved it when your grandmother would make us lunch and we would spend the whole day in the fields. Those were good times Cassandra. I loved every minute we spent together."

"Me too." Cassy reached across the seat and patted his hand. "Me too."

"You know this farm is a lot to handle. If something happens to me you know you inherit the entire thing?" James asked.

"Don't talk that way Grandfather. You'll be around for a long time to come."

"Cassandra we need to talk about this. I want you to know you don't have to hang on to the farm when I'm gone. I'm leaving it to you but that doesn't mean you have to live here and keep it running. There are lots of people around town who would love to buy it from you."

"I know. What if I promise you I'll think about it, seriously?"

"I guess that's all I can ask. I don't want you staying here because you feel like you have to. I want you to be happy. That's all I ever wanted for you."

"Thank you Grandfather. I promise if I'm not happy running the farm I'll sell it and find something else to do."

Cassy turned the truck off the gravel and onto a dirt road. "Can we still go this way for a little while and check out the fences?"

"Sure. When you get down to the end of this road take a right. I want to show you some of the things Gus Thompson and his sons have done to their farm house. You remember Gus' youngest, Tom, went to college and studied architecture?"

"I remember you telling me that."

"Well when he graduated he talked his other brother, Chad, who was working construction in

Dallas, into helping him remodel their parent's home." James chuckled. "Chad's now working with Gus here on the farm.

Cassy couldn't remember the last time she heard her grandfather laugh.

"I can't wait for you to see it. It looks like something from outer space. I can tell Gus hates it but would never say anything and hurt his sons' or wife's feelings. I hear he's taking a lot of ribbing about it when he goes into town."

Cassy turned right like her grandfather had asked.

"It's right up here." James pointed out the truck window.

"Is that it?" Cassy pulled into the driveway and headed closer to the house.

"Yep, that's it. What do you think?" James smiled

"You were right. It looks like a spaceship. Why would they let him change their house into that?" Cassy asked.

"James Conner."

Cassy heard a man's voice coming from the barn on the far end of the driveway.

"Hi Gus. What's new with you?" James asked.

Cassy waved to Gus. "Hello, Mr. Thompson." She stepped out of the truck to shake his hand.

"Welcome home Cassandra. I heard you were coming back to visit and maybe stay with your grandfather." Gus Thompson smiled.

"Yes, I am."

"That's great. So what are you two doing down this direction?" Gus asked.

"Grandfather wanted to show me your house. He said your sons did the remodeling." Cassy looked at her grandfather and his hand was fisted except for his thumb pointed straight up in the air. Cassy guessed she was covering nicely.

"So what do you think about it Cassy?" Gus asked.

"It's different Mr. Thompson. You must be proud."

"Yes ma'am. By the way James, I artificially inseminated my cows and everything is going great."

"I'm glad you're pleased Gus. Let me know when you decide to use my prize bull's services again."

"I will. That's the best two thousand dollars I've spent. I'll be in touch." Gus replied. "Would you like a tour of the house Cassandra?"

"If Grandfather and I weren't in a hurry to get back to the house I'd take you up on it."

"You come back anytime Cassandra and bring James." Gus nodded in James' direction.

"I'll do that. It was nice to see you again Mr. Thompson." Cassy climbed in the truck, backed out of the driveway headed home.

"You were right. That was the strangest looking house I've seen." Cassy noticed her grandfather had become very quiet.

"Are you all right?"

"Yes, I'm fine. I was just thinking about something. Let's head back home."

"I thought we were going to look at the rest of the farm?"

"We can finish up tomorrow. Right now I want to go back to the house and check out some paperwork."

"Something I can help with?" Cassy asked.

"Maybe. Right now I'm not sure what's going on myself."

****

Cassy helped her grandfather out of the truck and back into the house.

"It's about time for lunch. Would you like me to make you a sandwich? I'm a little hungry myself."

"I'd like that. How about a ham sandwich?" James asked as he sat down in his wheelchair and rolled into the front room. "Call me when it's ready."

"Sure." Cassy watched him roll up to his desk and start flipping through pages in two notebooks he had retrieved from his desk. She started making the sandwiches and tried to keep an eye on what he was doing. Pouring both of them a glass of iced tea, she put their sandwiches on the table then walked into the front room.

"Your sandwich is done. Are you ready to eat?"

"Sure. I'm starving." Cassy watched her grandfather close the notebooks and put them away in a desk drawer. She might just have to do some nosing around when he took his afternoon rest.

****

After finishing their sandwiches, Cassy helped her grandfather take his insulin shots and then cleaned up the kitchen.

"I think I'll go lay down for a little while. Have you got plans for the afternoon?" James asked.

"Nothing really. I have some emails to answer and I need to return some calls to my friends. I'll be around the house if you need me." Cassy gave her grandfather a kiss and helped him wheel into his bedroom and lay down on the bed.

"I was thinking we could have some soup and salad for dinner tonight. I'll make some beef stew. How does that sound?" Cassy adjusted the wheelchair so he could get out of bed when he woke from his nap.

"Sounds good to me."

"Have a nice rest."

Cassy headed back to the kitchen until her grandfather was sleeping then sat down at his desk to find the notebooks he was thumbing through earlier.

"Let's see what we can find." The pages were full of names, addresses, and phone numbers each seemed to have been given a special id number which, from what Cassy could tell, was an identifiable number. Across the top of the page was written A/I Clients.

Cassy knew the notes had something to do with his artificial Insemination clients because they were kept together with all the other books to do with the business of the farm. But what? She would have to question her grandfather a little further when he woke.

"Where's Mr. Conner."

Cassy was startled by Colt's voice from behind her.

"Colt, don't sneak up on me like that." Cassy placed her hand on her chest to make sure her heart didn't jump out. "You almost scared me to death."

"Sorry about that Cassy. I thought you would hear me when I opened the screen door. It has that squeak you can hear from anywhere."

"Grandfather is laying down to rest. What did you need?"

"I wanted to talk to him for a minute. I guess it can wait."

Cassy continued putting the books back where her grandfather kept them.

"What are you looking for?" Colt asked.

"Nothing really." Cassy reached back into the desk and took out the notebooks. "Wait, maybe you can help me."

"Sure, with what?"

Colt moved closer and leaned down to see what she had in her hands. Casey was having a hard time keeping her train of thought as he moved in just a little closer.

"We were out driving around the farm today. Grandfather wanted to show me the Thompson's new house. While we were there, Mr. Thompson and Grandfather were talking about the champion bull service. For some reason Grandfather became really quiet and wanted to head home."

"What's so strange about that?" Colt asked.

"I'm not sure but when we made it home Grandfather came straight in here and was thumbing through these notebooks like he was looking for something." Cassy handed the notebooks to Colt. "Is there something there you see that's out of place or strange?"

Cassy watched as Colt flipped through the pages.

"I don't see anything. Nothing at all." He handed the notebooks back to Cassy. "So he acted strange, huh? Did Gus say something to your grandfather?"

"Just that he was thinking about using the service again. It was the best two thousand dollars he had ever spent."

"Really? Huh, I don't think there's anything strange about that." Colt paused for a minute. "Would you tell Mr. Conner I need to go into town to get a part for the tractor? Since it's already afternoon, I'll probably grab dinner and a few beers in town so I'll be back a little after dark."

"Sure, I'll tell him." Cassy placed the notebooks back in the desk drawer.

"Also tell him I would like to sit down and talk to you two about the farm. When you can make some time, let me know."

"I'm sure we can make some time."

"Great. Is there anything you need while I'm in town? I'll be happy to pick it up for you."

"I think there might be a few things. Thanks for asking." Cassy stood up from the desk. "Let me get you some money and a list."

She found the list on the kitchen cabinet and took some money out of the cookie jar where her grandfather showed her he kept it and handed it to Colt.

"That should be enough."

"If you guys are already in bed when I get home, I'll slip in and put them on the cabinet."

"Sounds good. Just make sure to lock the door when you leave."

"Lock the door? You can't take the City out of the girl." Colt smiled and nodded. "I'll see you tomorrow then. Have a good evening."

"Thanks. Have fun in town. Try to stay out of trouble since you can't take the country out of the boy." Cassy smiled and watched as Colt ran his fingers through his thick, black hair and put on his cowboy hat.

"Now, that wouldn't be any fun would it?"

A stream of heat ran through her body as Colt gave her a quick wink and smile. She was sure there had to be plenty of women in town willing to share an evening with Colt Matthews. Cassy was taken by surprise when she suddenly felt a twinge of jealousy rush through her body.

****

"Dinner was wonderful Cassy."

"Thanks Grandfather. Grandmother taught me everything I know." Cassy picked up the dishes from the table and put them in the sink.

"You know she loved having you here. You were like the daughter she never had. I don't know if your grandmother ever told you that she always wanted a big family but she had problems when she carried your father. After she had him, the doctors told her she wouldn't be able to have any more kids." James took a sip of his iced tea.

"Grandmother never told me. I guess I never questioned why she only had one child. She loved children so much."

"She was pretty upset for a long time and then you came along. You were what she needed to forget her despair over the situation. She was the happiest I had ever seen her."

Cassy noticed a tear in the corner of her grandfather's eye.

"Thank you for telling me that Grandfather." She gave him a hug. "I loved her too."

"Sure. Now, how about you help me take my shots?" James wheeled over to the cabinet to get his insulin then back to the table.

"It would be my pleasure." Cassy pulled a chair up next to him and watched as he took the needle and carefully filled it with insulin.

"That should be just about right with what we had for dinner. You agree?"

"Let's see, you had a pretty big bowl of stew and a salad. That should be just right." Cassy smiled. "Can I give you the shot?"

"Here you go."

Cassy took the needle from her grandfather and watched as he lifted the tail of his shirt. She gave him his shot then broke the needle off the syringe and tossed them both in a special safety container to keep them out of the regular trash. "That should do it. Now I'm going to finish cleaning up the kitchen."

"I think I'll go into the front room and do some reading. I'll let you know before I turn in for the night."

"By the way Grandfather, before I forget, Colt wanted to sit down with the two of us and talk. Something about the farm. I told him we could make some time."

"We can make some time tomorrow. About the farm huh? I wonder what it is."

"I have no idea. I guess we'll find out tomorrow. I am going outside and enjoy the evening. How about if we have some milk and cookies before you go to bed?" Cassy asked as he wheeled into the living room through the kitchen door.

"Sounds wonderful."

"Okay. Go ahead. Leave me alone here to talk to myself. I'll be fine, don't worry." Cassy replied under her breath continuing to clean the kitchen. "This house will be spotless unless I find some other things to do in this town."

7

"Hey, Colt." A voice from behind caused him to turn around.

"Lucas." Colt spotted him walking towards him. "What's up?"

"I could ask you the same. It's not normal for you to be in town at night during the week. What errand does old-man Conner have you doing now?" Lucas sat down at the table.

"He doesn't. I had some personal business to take care of." Colt was never quite sure about Lucas but he had grown to like him over the past few months. He knew his stuff and seemed to care about James Conner when he answered emergency calls at the farm. Being a paramedic seemed to be a profession he was good at. Colt took the last drink of his beer and sat the glass down on the table.

"So how is the old man doing since our last visit? Is his granddaughter helping take care of his diabetes? What was her name? Cassy?" Lucas asked.

"He's doing better. Cassy is trying to learn and help him. She'll get there."

"So how is it for you to have her around? Are you adjusting to having a woman for a boss now?" Lucas laughed.

"She's not my boss. Not yet. I still answer to Mr. Conner." Colt wasn't sure how he was going to handle Cassy as a boss when the time came. "I guess I'll worry about it when it happens."

"She seems really business-like. Nice looking but business-like. I wonder what she knows about running a farm."

"I'm not sure what she knows. I don't know how to tell her she is taking on a headache."

"What do you mean? I thought the Conner farm was doing great. Especially since you guys started earning fees for those prize winning bulls old man Conner has."

"Mr. Conner ran up quite a few bills after his wife died and then his health went downhill. While he was taking care of all his medical expenses, I was worrying about the farm." Colt replied.

"So you're saying the farm is losing money?"

"It was. I pumped some of my personal money into the farm to keep it afloat until Mr. Conner could get back on his feet. I'm working on getting my money back now we are making a profit. I have to talk to Mr. Conner and Cassy tomorrow and explain what I have done and see how they react."

"They should be thankful you were there to help him out. Why didn't you call his family and let them worry about it?"

"Cassy was the only family I knew of and I had no idea how to find her. When Mr. Conner was sick I couldn't get any information out of him. Using my own funds was all I could think of to keep from him losing everything and me losing my job."

"So how have you been repaying yourself and him not know? Doesn't the old man keep an eye on the books?"

"I've been raising the fee we are charging for the champion bull fees and taking the difference as payback. Problem is I think the old man figured it out today. I need to talk to him before he gets the wrong idea."

"Why would he get the wrong idea?"

"He might think I'm cheating him and skimming money by raising the fees. He doesn't understand he was way underpriced in the market. The customers were willing to pay the extra. They didn't even blink an eye. I kept the price where I wasn't ripping anyone off."

"I think the old man will understand when you explain it to him. Cassy on the other hand might need some convincing." Lucas chuckled. "Let me know if you need some help with her. She looks like a handful."

"I'll be fine. Cassy is a nice girl. You just have to get to know her."

"I'd like to get to know her. I'd like to get to know her a lot better. I've been thinking about asking her out for dinner. I'm looking forward to seeing what she's got to offer."

Colt changed the subject quickly. A raging fire was starting in the pit of his stomach and he was getting angry with Lucas for talking about Cassy that way. For some reason, he felt a strange need to protect her. He had enough on his mind. He didn't need to add having words with Lucas over Cassy. He caught the eye of his the waitress and motioned for her.

"Can we get a picture of what's on draft please?" Colt asked.

"It's on me." Lucas handed the waitress a twenty.

"Thanks Lucas. I had a little too much coffee after dinner and a few beers. Nature calls. I'll be right back." Colt excused himself.

"I'll grab us a pool table."

****

Lucas checked out the young waitress as she sat down the pitcher of beer with two clean glasses and his change.

"Thanks. Keep the change."

Lucas touched her on the arm running his hand lightly up and down her bare skin. "Why don't I hang around until you get off? Maybe we can spend some time together."

"What about your friend?" The waitress leaned against him smiling.

"You don't worry about him. He'll be leaving soon." Lucas reached around and grabbed a handful of her buttocks then patted her playfully.

"I'll see what I can do about getting off early." She laughed as she turned to leave.

"Good girl." Lucas smiled as he watched her walk away. "Nice. Now to take care of my good friend Colt."

****

Still full from dinner Cassy passed on the cookies and milk with her grandfather before bed. She decided to turn in early so she helped her grandfather to his room, gave him a glass of milk and a few cookies and left his insulin case by his bed for him to take his nightly shot.

She slipped her nightgown on, folded her clothes and put them away then took a few minutes to brush her hair and teeth before she climbed under the covers. Flipping through the channels on the television she found a show she wanted to watch and settled in bed. It didn't take very long before she was asleep only to be awaken by noises coming from downstairs. Turning off the television, Cassy listened for more sounds. She heard another noise which seemed to be coming from the kitchen. She looked at the clock which read twelve thirty. Cassy slipped on her bathrobe and then tip-toed down the stairs until she reached the bottom. Carefully peaking around the corner, she noticed Colt placing bags on the kitchen cabinet.

"A little after dark. Whatever. He must have found something or someone fun to keep him in town."

She didn't feel like carrying on a conversation so she quietly headed back upstairs to her room. Climbing back into bed she covered back up and went back to sleep.

Cassy opened her eyes and glanced at the clock. The sun wasn't quite up and she was awake. *It didn't take long for my internal clock to kick in and reset to the crack of dawn.*

Stretching her body and climbing out of bed, Cassy brushed her hair, slipped on her bathrobe and headed downstairs to start breakfast. She glanced in her grandfather's bedroom in passing and noticed he wasn't awake.

"Good Morning." Colt walked through the back door and took off his hat laying it on the table. "Where's the old man? He's usually up and waiting for me in the morning."

"I was just going to check. I walked by his bedroom and it didn't look like he was awake which isn't like him at all." Cassy turned and ran into his bedroom

"Grandfather." She sat down on the bed. This time was different. He looked so peaceful. If Cassy didn't know better she could swear he was smiling. She looked at the clock and it read five minutes after six."

"Call 911." She looked up at Colt with tears running down her cheeks. "See if Lucas is on duty and if he can take the call."

Colt picked up the phone and dialed as Cassy held her grandfather's hand. She listened as Colt gave all the information to the operator.

"They're on the way. Is he....?" Colt couldn't manage to say the word.

"Yes, I think so." Cassy could feel the tears flowing. She wasn't ready to let him go. She felt Colt sit down on the bed behind her and put his arms on her shoulders.

"I'm sorry Cassy. I'm really sorry."

Cassy couldn't say anything for what seemed an eternity. Everything was so quiet until she heard the sirens in the distance. Colt headed for the door to let them in.

"Cassy." Lucas helped her up from the bed and handed her to Colt to steady. "I need to check him out."

Cassy watched as Lucas tried to find a pulse then checked his breathing. He pulled a flashlight out of his pocket and checked his eyes. He stood up and took Cassy in his arms.

"I'm sorry Cassy. He's gone. It looks like he's been gone for a few hours now."

All she could do was cry. Her knees became weak and her heart began to pound faster. She sat down in the closest chair and wept. Years of memories they shared flashed before her eyes.

"Why don't we go in the kitchen and maybe have some coffee. The Coroner and the ambulance are right behind me. They'll take Mr. Conner to the morgue then release him to the funeral home. I'm sure they will want to talk to you."

Lucas helped her up and steadied her as they headed for the kitchen. Cassy took one last look at her grandfather before she walked out of his bedroom.

"He looks so peaceful."

"Yes he does. I don't think I've seen him smile like that except when he would talk about you." Lucas replied.

"I'm going to miss him so much. I can't believe he's gone." Cassy replied.

"He knew you loved him. His life was complete with you here. It will take time but everything will be all right. You wait and see."

Cassy sat down in the chair at the table and watched Lucas make his way around the kitchen finding the coffee and filters.

"Was there anything different about him last night? Did he have any problems or seem ill?" Lucas asked.

"No, we had dinner, he took his shot and then he did some reading in the front room. He had milk and cookies before we went to bed. I was too full from dinner so I passed on the milk and cookies." Cassy began to cry again. "I should have had milk and cookies with him."

"You had no idea Cassy. Don't think like that." Colt put his hand on her shoulder to try and comfort her.

"After that, he checked his blood and then we both turned in. Nothing different at all." Cassy replied.

"I'm sure there will be an autopsy and we'll find out exactly what happened. It could have been his heart or anything. I wish I could tell you more but I just don't know for sure."

"I know you are doing the best you can. Thank you for everything Lucas."

"How about you Colt, did you notice anything strange about Mr. Conner last night?"

"No, but I wasn't here. I went into town yesterday and didn't return until after midnight. Everything seemed quiet and normal when I got home." Colt replied. "If you're all right Cassy, I'm going to go outside and watch for the ambulance."

"Sure, go ahead." Cassy hadn't thought about how hard this must be on Colt. He had worked for her grandfather for over five years now. He had to be hurting also and wondering what is going to happen now.

"Colt, wait." Cassy said. "Thank you for being here."

"Sure Cassy. I'm sorry about Mr. Conner. It's been my pleasure working for him these past five years. It's not going to be the same around here."

Cassy could swear she heard Colt's voice cracking. She couldn't tell for sure because he was out the door before he finished his sentence.

8

    Cassy still couldn't believe her grandfather was gone. The house was lonely and quiet. She wasn't sure what to do now. She had moved here to help her grandfather out on the farm. Now that he was gone she was not only alone on the farm but now the owner.
    Lucas wanted to meet her in town to make sure arrangements were made for her grandfather's funeral. She was also going to take clothes for him to be buried in. She had argued with Colt about what clothes to choose. Colt wanted to take a suit and Cassy felt a nice shirt and slacks would look more like him. She didn't remember her grandfather wearing a suit except for a few times in her life. He seemed very uncomfortable each time. How could she make him wear one for eternity? The last thing she wanted was to be buried in a dress.
    "What a horrible thought."
    "What's a horrible thought?"
    Cassy turned around to see Colt standing in the kitchen.
    "Nothing, I was talking to myself."

"Are you all right?" Colt asked. "I thought I would stop by and see if you needed anything."

"Thank you Colt but I'm fine." Cassy paused for a minute. "I'll be fine. It's going to take a while."

"I know what you mean. I expect to see him come wheeling out of the bedroom."

"Me too." Cassy watched as Colt took off his hat and sat down at the kitchen table.

"So how long are you going to stay here? Now that your grandfather is gone I expect you'll want to sell the ranch and move back to the City."

"What makes you say that Colt?" Cassy looked surprised by his question.

"There's nothing keeping you here now. All your family is gone. I just thought."

"You think I am going to move away. Do you think I'm going to sell the farm?" Cassy asked. "Maybe sell it to you?"

"Not at all." Colt stuttered. "That's not at all what I was thinking. I know you have friends in the City and I thought you might want to be close to them instead of stickin' around here where you don't know many people." Colt threw his shoulders back. "And what would be wrong with selling the farm to me?"

"Nothing." Cassy replied. "I appreciate you thinking about my future but I believe I'm going to stay. I like it here."

"Do you like it here because of the farm or do you like it here because of Lucas?"

"What do you mean by that?"

"You'd have to be blind to not see the sparks flying when you and Lucas are together." Colt laughed.

"Lucas and I are just friends. I don't know what you're talking about, sparks." Cassy didn't understand if Colt could see sparks when she and Lucas were together, what did he see when she looked at him?

"Right. Go ahead and play dumb. Even your grandfather mentioned it."

"He never said anything to me." Cassy replied. "Let's change the subject if you don't mind."

"Whatever you say." Colt stood up and headed for the backdoor. "I have to go back to work."

"Have a great day Colt." Cassy watched him wave and walk out the door.

"Sparks, huh? You have no idea about sparks. I'll show you sparks."

****

The service for James Conner was packed. It seems as if everyone in town had shown up to express their condolences. Cassy hadn't seen this many people at once since she left the City. She was glad the service was over but now came settling down on the farm without him around.

"Cassy." A voice came from behind her. "Wait a minute. I want to talk to you."

She watched as Lucas tried to make his way around the crowd towards her.

"Lucas. What's going on?"

"I wanted to talk to you for a minute. Do you have the time?" Lucas asked

"Of course. What do you want to talk about?"

"I have to get back to work soon and I wanted to see if you would like have dinner with me next week." Lucas paused for a minute. "I'm sorry Cassy. I wasn't thinking. I know this is a hard time for you. I can't believe I'm asking you out to dinner at your grandfather's funeral but I didn't know when I would see you again."

"It's all right Lucas. I would like to have dinner with you."

"Why don't I call you in the next few days and we'll make arrangements?"

"That's sounds great. I'll look forward to it."

Cassy made her way around the room after Lucas left. She was lost without her grandfather. This was one time she was thankful for both Lucas and Colt. Since she didn't have any family left, they would be the closest thing.

9

Cassy was surprised by knocking at the front door.

"Who would come to the front door? Nobody ever comes to the front door." She put the dish towel down on the cabinet and headed through the living room to open the door.

"Ms. Cassandra Conner?"

Cassy didn't know what to say or think. The older gentleman in a wrinkled suit was standing at the door looked heated from the afternoon sun. A younger man behind him was fanning himself with a manila folder.

"Yes. Can I help you?"

"I'm Detective Sloan and this is Detective Rogers." The older gentleman flipped open a black leather wallet containing his badge. "May we come in?"

"Yes, of course. " Cassy stepped aside and let the two men enter the living room. They both stopped right inside the door.

"What can I do for you?" Cassy asked.

"We would like to ask you some questions about your grandfather's death. Can we sit down?"

"I'm sorry. Where are my manners?" Cassy pointed to the couch and chair. "Please have a seat. Can I get you something to drink? Some iced tea or water?"

"Some water would be good." Detective Sloan replied.

"Same for me please." Detective Rogers replied.

"I'll be right back." Cassy walked into the kitchen and poured two glasses of water from the pitcher in the refrigerator and handed them to the men.

"What can I answer for you about my grandfather's death?" Cassy asked. "I thought everything was covered when I talked the Coroner and Detective who were here the night Grandfather passed away."

"We were called after the coroner received the results of the autopsy. We believe your grandfather's death wasn't from natural causes."

"What do you mean?" Cassy asked. "I just assumed his heart gave out. It wasn't in the best of shape because of his diabetes."

"According to the Coroner's report his diabetes was the cause of his death but we believe he had some help."

"What exactly are you getting at Detective Sloan?" Cassy asked.

"We believe, whether by accident or on purpose, your grandfather took the wrong insulin. We need to find out exactly what happened that night so we can put this question to rest."

"What do you mean the wrong insulin? You think Grandfather either took the wrong insulin by accident or somebody switched his insulin?" Cassy laughed. "I can't believe that. I was sitting right beside him when he took his shot after dinner. I helped him measure the dose and he even let me give him the shot. I've been practicing just in case."

"In case what?" Detective Rogers finally piped in.

"In case my grandfather got sick or was somehow incapable of giving himself his own shots. I needed to know how much he took, when, why. All the important information."

"So you knew what type of insulin he took, when and how much to give him?"

"Yes. I was working with my grandfather and Lucas Harding. Lucas was teaching me how to count the carbohydrates Grandfather ate and how much insulin he took as a result. I learned he took Humalog after each meal because it was the quick acting insulin and before bed he would take Lantus which is the long acting insulin that kept his blood sugars down during the night."

"It sounds like you have quite a bit of knowledge on the subject. In fact, you would have enough knowledge you could switch your grandfather's insulin and cause him to go into a diabetic coma." Detetive Sloan stated.

"That's crazy. I would never do that or even think of doing that." Cassy exclaimed. "I really don't appreciate you insinuating I would do anything of the kind."

"The results of the Coroner's report show your grandfather slipped into a diabetic coma as a result of too much insulin. I understand from the logs at the EMT station there have been several calls to this address because your grandfather had problems with his blood sugar being too low. Am I right?" Detective Sloan read from a notebook he pulled from his pocket. "I can give you the dates if you would like."

"No, it's not necessary. Yes, my grandfather had one spell since I've come back to the farm. The first day I was here. He laid down to rest and his blood sugar was low because he hadn't eaten lunch. We had to call the paramedics. Luckily Lucas Harding was on duty. He is very familiar with my grandfather and his diabetes. Or I should say he was very familiar." Cassy paused for a minute. "The next time we called the paramedics was the night my grandfather passed away. Those are the only two times I'm aware of."

"So tell me exactly what happened the night your grandfather passed. Please don't leave anything out." Detective Rogers said.

"Fine. I'll do my best." Cassy paused for a minute trying to calm down enough to remember as much as she could about that night. "My grandfather and I ate breakfast. He took his shots while I cleaned up the kitchen. We took a ride around the farm. He wanted to show me some of the new projects. We ran into a neighbor down the road and we drove down to see his newly remodeled house."

"You mean the Thompson's? What do you think about that remodeling job? It's a good thing it was their son who was responsible or I'd have to shoot the designer." Detective Rogers laughed.

"Continue Ms. Conner. What happened after that?" Detective Sloan shot a disapproving look at Detective Rogers.

"Sorry." Detective Rogers replied.

"After we left the Thompson's we came home and had lunch. Grandfather was doing some work at the desk while I fixed him a sandwich. He ate then laid down for a little while. I cleaned up the lunch dishes. Colt came in looking for Grandfather. We talked for a few minutes and then he took a list and some money because he was going into town for supplies. Grandfather woke up and we had dinner, he read some in the living room then went to bed and I went upstairs to watch television. I fell asleep. I remember waking up to a noise."

"What noise was that?"

"It was Colt. He had gotten home from town and was putting the supplies he bought in the kitchen. I returned to my room and went back to sleep. The next thing I knew it was morning. I came downstairs to check on Grandfather and make breakfast. That's when I found him. Colt had come in before and he was with me when we found him. He called 911 and you know everything after that."

"So no one else was alone with your grandfather the day he died?" Detective Sloan asked.

"No. Grandfather and I were together most of the day. The only time I wasn't with him was after dinner when I was upstairs watching television."

"Could anyone else have come by to visit while you were upstairs?"

"I would have heard if someone had come to visit. I don't believe so. The only other person who has free run of the house is Colt and like I told you he was in town buying supplies. He didn't get home until after we had gone to bed."

"Are you sure about when he returned home?" Detective Rogers asked.

"I woke up around twelve thirty. That's when I heard the noise. I slipped downstairs and Colt was in the kitchen putting supplies away. I assume he had just gotten home."

"Thank you, Ms. Conner, for your time." Detective's Sloan and Rogers both stood up at the same time as each handed Cassy a business card. "I'm sure we'll need to talk to you again. Please let us know if you leave town."

Cassy stood up and walked to the front door with the two detectives. She wasn't sure what else to say or if she should even say anything else but she had to know.

"Do you think my grandfather was murdered?"

"We really don't want to speculate Ms. Conner. The evidence will speak for itself if we give it time."

That line sounded to Cassy like one some television detective would use. She needed to find out what was going on. *Lucas.* He would tell her exactly what these two were thinking and digging for.

10

"Hello." Lucas answered his cell.

"Lucas. It's Cassy Conner. I hope I didn't catch you at a bad time."

"No. Not at all." This was a nice surprise. He didn't expect to hear from her for a few days.

"Good. I need to ask you a question." Cassy continued. "I had two Detectives visit me this afternoon. They were asking questions about the day my grandfather passed away. They told me they didn't think my grandfather died of natural causes."

"Really. What else did they say?' Lucas asked.

"They said he died of taking too much insulin or the wrong kind. They believe someone either gave him too much or switched his insulin. Can you help me understand what they are talking about?"

"I'll answer your questions the best I can. I'm off work right now. Why don't I come over and we can talk."

"Thank you, Lucas. I really need your help to understand this."

As Lucas hung up the phone he smirked "Of course you need my help Cassy. I bet you do." He couldn't help but feel her soft auburn hair, and long sexy legs weren't going to keep her out of trouble. Too bad they were wasted on him.

Lucas pulled up to the Conner farm. The lights were on inside. He watched Cassy moving around the kitchen.

"You are going to have to be careful Lucas boy." The police detectives had already talked to him since he had been one of the responders the night James Conner died. Stepping out of the truck he greeted Cassy as she walked out of the back door of the house.

"Hi Cassy."

"Lucas. Thanks for coming over."

"Sure." Lucas walked up to meet her at the door.

"Come in. It's cooler in the house."

Watching her walk back into the house, Lucas realized how attractive Cassy Conner was. He was sure she attracted a lot of attention when she was out on the town but that wasn't what he found interesting about her. He had never met a woman who made him feel challenged. Cassy Conner was one woman he had to watch himself around.

"I made some tea or I have beer. What can I get you?" Cassy asked.

"A glass of iced tea." Lucas sat down at the kitchen table. "So, you mentioned the detectives paid you a visit. What exactly did they tell you?"

"They think Grandfather's death wasn't natural causes."

"So what made them think that?" Lucas asked.

"The results of the autopsy showed Grandfather died with too much insulin in his body which made his blood sugar go down. That sent him into a coma which he never came out of." Cassy joined Lucas at the table placing two glasses of iced tea in front of them.

"So how do they think your grandfather received too much insulin?"

"They are saying he received too much insulin or his insulin was switched and he took the wrong kind. I was hoping you could explain to me why they think that."

Lucas couldn't help but wonder what was going through that pretty little head of hers as Cassy leaned back in her chair crossing her legs at the knee.

"I was learning how much he needed to take but I don't know all the side effects of too much insulin versus too little or the wrong kinds versus the right."

"So what they are saying is he could have been given or taken the wrong insulin in his nightly shot." Lucas took a sip of his tea. "If what they are saying is right, they probably think someone switched his fast acting with his long acting insulin. That would make his blood sugar go down very fast and put him in a coma."

"There was no one else around the day Grandfather died. Colt and I were the only two people. Colt left in the afternoon to go into town. He didn't get back until after midnight."

"So that only leaves you." Lucas looked as her expression changed to one of confusion.

"I could never do anything like they are saying. I loved my grandfather. I could have never even let a thought like that enter my head."

Tears began to roll down her checks. Lucas couldn't help himself. He reached up and wiped one away.

"I'm sure this will all be straightened out. The detectives will figure out what happened that night and everything will be all right."

"You think so?" Cassy asked.

"I'm sure of it." Lucas smiled. "We might have to give them some help but they will figure it out."

"What do you mean? Give them some help."

"I'm not quite sure yet." Lucas replied. "I'll let you know when I figure it out."

"Thanks for coming over Lucas." Cassy reached out and touched his hand. "I don't know what I would have done if you hadn't come over. This is all I can think about and hanging around this big empty house alone doesn't help my thought process."

"I'm glad I could help." Lucas knew he couldn't let himself develop any kind of feelings for Cassy. There was too much at stake. He wasn't sure he could help her or whether he should. After all, most of the people around town were talking and they were sure she was guilty of her grandfather's death. Maybe he should leave it that way.

11

    Colt stood back inside the barn as he watched Lucas walk out the back door of the house with Cassy following close behind him.
    "Well, well. Isn't that cozy? Old man Conner isn't even warm in his grave and she's entertaining gentlemen."
    He watched as Lucas climbed into his truck and drove off. Cassy stood off to the side watching him drive away and then walked back in the house.
    "I guess it's about time Cassy and I had a talk. First the Detectives and now Lucas. I better find out exactly what's going on." He put away the tools he was working with in the barn and headed towards the house.
    He could see Cassy in the kitchen. He made some noise walking up to the house so he wouldn't scare her when he walked in the door.
    "Hi Cassy." Colt took his hat off and hung it from the back of the chair. "Was that Lucas I just saw leaving?"
    "Yes, it was Lucas." Cassy replied. "I'm going to make myself a sandwich for dinner. Would you

like something? I'll be happy to leave everything out."

"Sure. I'll make myself something since you have it out." Colt walked over to the sink and washed his hands.

"So what did Lucas have to say? Anything important? He didn't want to stay for dinner?" Colt tried not to make it too obvious he was just a little jealous.

"Not much. He had to get back because he works a shift tonight. He was talking to me about the night Grandfather passed." Cassy placed her sandwich plate down on the table and filled a glass with tea. "Did I tell you I had a visit from a couple of Detectives?"

"No, you didn't. What did they want?" Colt kept his back to Cassy so she couldn't see his reaction. She didn't need to know he already knew they had visited because he had been watching her.

"They had some questions about Grandfather's death." Cassy replied.

"What kind of questions?" Colt took his sandwich and sat down at the table with Cassy.

"According to the Coroner's report, Grandfather didn't die of natural causes."

"No way. What did they say he died of?" Colt asked.

"They seem to think he had some help. He had too much fast acting insulin in his blood stream."

"So exactly what does that mean?" Colt took a bite of his sandwich while he listened.

"He accidently took the wrong insulin or..." Cassy paused.

"Or what?" Colt asked.

Or someone switched his insulin before he took his nightly shot."

"They told you that?"

"Yeah. They pretty much accused me of killing my grandfather."

"That's crazy."

"They don't seem to think so. I was the only one with him most of the day. You were in town buying supplies and didn't get home until late."

"How do you know what time I got home?" Colt acted surprised by Cassy's remark.

"I woke up when you were putting the supplies away in the kitchen. I assumed you were just getting home."

"Oh, yes. Yes I was just getting home. I didn't think I woke anyone." Colt replied.

"Anyway, I guess I'm the only logical person."

"Did the Detectives say what they were going to do about this?"

"Not really. They just said they were still looking into the evidence and they would get back to me. I guess I'm their prime suspect because I was given the 'Don't leave town' line."

"Wow, I've never known anyone accused of murder. You don't look the type." Colt laughed.

"Not funny Colt. Knock it off." Cassy seemed upset by his remark as she grabbed her plate and rinsed it off and placed it in the sink.

"I'm sorry Cassy. I didn't mean to upset you. I understand this has to be hard for you knowing they might think you had something to do with your grandfather's death." Colt walked over to the sink and put his hand on her arms. "I'm here for you if you need me. Just let me know what you need."

Colt could feel Cassy's body tense up as his closeness became apparent to her. He was enjoying the feel of her soft skin beneath his hands and found her attractive. Touching her made him realize how she was very defensive. Still, he wouldn't mind at all knowing what the rest of her body felt like beneath his touch. He was going to have to make her feel more secure. He was also going to have to take it slow and gain her confidence.

"I'll be fine Colt. Don't worry about me."

His thoughts were interrupted by her sudden determination to be strong and independent. He knew if he was going to pursue her he would have to find a way to break through the barrier he could feel between them. "Well at least I have you as an alibi."

"What are you talking about?" Cassy pulled away from his grip as she turned to face him. "Your alibi?"

"Yeah. You know a person who can vouch for where you were and all that stuff."

"I'm not your alibi. You weren't here with Grandfather and me. You were in town buying supplies."

"Exactly. There's no way I could have had anything to do with your grandfather's death. I was in town buying supplies." Colt smiled. "You're my alibi and a beautiful one at that."

Colt couldn't resist kissing her. There was a fire in her eyes. She was right there. Her body was close enough he could feel the warmth of her skin next to his. Her lips were soft and wet just like he imagined. The kiss didn't last long as Cassy pushed him away.

"What are you doing?"

"Kissing you. Haven't you ever been kissed before?" Colt held on tight to her arms.

"Let me go Colt. That was totally out of line." Cassy exclaimed.

"Are you sure? I think you liked it." He felt Cassy pull her arms free of his grip and move away.

Colt wasn't sure but he thought for a minute she might hit him.

"Why don't you leave?" Cassy pointed at the back door.

"Come on Cassy. Don't be mad. How long's it been since you had a man kiss you?" Colt moved towards her but stopped in his tracks when he felt the sting of her hand across his face.

"I said leave. Now!" The expression on her face told him everything he needed to know.

"Sure. I'll leave. Let me know if you change your mind."

"Don't worry, I won't."

Colt picked up his cowboy hat off the back of the chair, combed his fingers through his hair then put his hat on his head. "You know where to find me." Frustrated by her behavior, he slammed the door behind him. "Women."

****

Cassy couldn't believe what just happened. *How could he have thought she enjoyed him kissing her? What did she do to make him think it would be all right?*

Cassy ran upstairs. She needed to take a bath, anything to get the thought of him out of her head. She was just as disgusted with herself as much as she was with Colt. She actually did enjoy his kiss, the feel of his lips on her. It had been a long time since she had been kissed by a man. He was right and the thought made her have a knot it the pit of her stomach.

"Don't go there Cassy." She grabbed her bathrobe and started the water in the bathtub. This time she was locking the bathroom doors and shutting the world out.

Sliding down into the bubbles of the bathtub she closed her eyes and Colt was there. His mouth pressed against her. She could feel his firm body and smell his scent as plain now as when it happened. The sensation was overtaking her. She didn't want to like the feeling but she knew she wanted it to happen again.

****

Cassy slipped on a nightgown and her robe and headed downstairs for a glass of milk before she turned in for the night. Her body was finally making the adjustment of getting up early and going to bed after the evening news. She didn't think her life would ever be routine like it was now. She poured her glass of milk, drank it and walked outside. The sky was perfectly clear and stars were visible from every piece of the sky. She sat down in the swing along the side of the house enjoying the cool breeze of the evening.

"I'm sorry about what happened in the kitchen earlier." Colt's voice came from out of the darkness.

She caught a glimpse of his outline as he came closer to her. She enjoyed what she saw. The closer he moved towards her, the stronger she could feel her body react. She caught the smell of soap and musk. He must have just showered and shaved. Not only did he have a sensuous air about him but the scent of him made her blood pulse through her body at a rapid speed.

"I hope I didn't upset you."

"Let's forget about it Colt." Cassy replied. "I'm sorry I got so upset." She slid over on the swing giving him enough room to sit down beside her. "You were right by the way."

"Right about what?" Colt put his arm across the back of the swing making heat flow deeper through her body. She wanted him to touch her, to take her upstairs and make love to her. She wanted to feel all of him next to her. Cassy knew she had to be careful what she shared with Colt. The idea of him was strong in Cassy and she knew in the right situation she was lost.

"It has been a long time since I was kissed by a man." Cassy looked down and fidgeted with a string on her robe. "But, that didn't make it all right for you to kiss me."

"I'll never figure you women out." Colt laughed.

"We aren't that difficult Colt. You guys just make it harder than it has to be."

"So you could give me a crash course?" Colt asked.

"Just treat us like you want to be treated. If you're nice and respectful we respond." Cassy looked at him thinking how much she wanted him to try and kiss her again.

"So what about my kissing you wasn't nice or respectful? I was using my best moves." Colt laughed.

"Those were you best moves?" Cassy laughed. "You and I have a lot of work to do."

"What if we start right now?"

Cassy was overwhelmed by his scent and feel as he pulled her close to him kissing her. At first, softly touching his lips on hers then covering her mouth completely with his, pressing his moist hot lips on hers. He was wonderful and his breath was warm and intoxicating. This time Cassy couldn't push away. She couldn't breathe. It was as if his kiss was taking the life out of her and replacing it with a sensuous, relaxing flow of warmth over her entire body. She melted into him.

Against her wishes Colt pulled his lips away from hers bringing her back to reality. She could hear her heart beating in her chest. She took a few seconds to catch her breath.

"How was that?"

"Well, let's see. If I was going to rate that kiss versus the one earlier I would say this one was an eight."

"Just an eight?" Colt pulled her closer to him leaving no room between them, kissing her with a passion she had never felt before. His hands caressed her body making himself familiar with the curves of her body.

"Colt." Cassy reluctantly managed to pull herself away and take a breath. "I think we need to stop right here."

"But Cassy, I respect you and I know you're enjoying this as much as I am."

"I'm not saying I'm not enjoying it. We have to work together Colt. I don't think this is a good idea." Cassy adjusted her robe and stood up from the swing. Colt stood up next to her. "Good night. I'll see you tomorrow."

"Good night Cassy." Colt gave her a peck on the cheek and patted her firm buttocks with his hand. "You know where to find me if you change your mind."

Cassy watched as he walked away back to the barn. Knowing where to find him could be a bad, bad thing for her.

****

Rinsing her face in the bathroom sink, Cassy looked at her reflection in the mirror. There were still dark circles under her eyes even though she had slept in a little longer than usual. Getting to sleep last night was hard when she couldn't stop thinking about Colt and his intoxicating kisses. After managing to drift off to sleep, he invaded her dreams. She tossed and turned all night.

"What are you getting yourself into?"

Cassy didn't have a chance to go any further with her thoughts because they were interrupted by her cell phone ringing.

"Hello."

"Cassy, it's Lucas Harding."

"Good morning Lucas. How are you?"

"Listen Cassy, I was wondering if you could meet me in town this morning. I want to talk to you about our conversation yesterday. I think I might have some information."

"Sure I can meet you. When and where?"

"Can you drive into town? How about at the City Café around noon? Would that work for you?"

"I'll meet you there."

"And Cassy."

"Yes Lucas."

"Would you come alone? I don't want Colt to know what you are up to."

"Why?" Cassy began to feel strange about this meeting. What was it exactly Lucas wanted to tell her.

"I'll explain when you get here. See you at noon."

Cassy ended the call and put her cell phone down on the night stand. "What am I going to tell Colt? He's going to want to know why I'm going into town."

Cassy slipped on a pair of jeans, pulled her hair back and put on a light touch of make up to cover the dark circles. She glanced at the clock.

She had just enough time to make it into town by noon. She grabbed her purse and headed for the back door.

"Good morning sunshine."

Cassy heard Colt's voice coming from the barn.

"Going somewhere?"

Cassy turned to catch a glimpse of Colt throwing bales of hay into the back of his truck. He was shirtless, sweaty and buff.

"Oh, man." Cassy whispered under her breath.

"Good morning Colt." She threw her purse in the front seat of the truck. "I've got to go into town. I just remembered I have an appointment I'm going to be late for."

"Do you need me to go with you? I can make it into town faster than anyone in the county."

"I don't think you want to go with me for this appointment." She hated lying to him but she couldn't tell him the truth. Lucas had asked her not to.

"Why?" Colt walked out the barn pushing his cowboy hat up on his forehead with his gloved finger.

"Let's just say it's a woman thing. I'll see you when I get back."

"Then why don't I plan on us having dinner together?"

Colt moved closer to her and kissed her on the cheek. He was so damn sexy. Hot, sweaty and gorgeous. Lucas better have something good to tell her.

"Sure. That sounds great. I'll see you when I get back."

"Drive safe." Colt waved as she headed down the drive.

"That was close. I'll have to make sure and thank Lucas for putting me in that awkward position. I wish I knew what this was all about."

12

  Cassy pulled into an empty parking spot outside the café. Lucas was standing by the door waiting for her.

  "Cassy." He waved as she climbed out of the truck.

  "Hi Lucas. How are you?"

  "Okay." He opened the door to the café motioning for Cassy to enter first. "Let's go in and sit down."

  "What's going on Lucas? You sounded like it was really important." Cassy followed him to a table and sat down across from him waving at Fannie across the room whose eyes she could feel burning holes. It wouldn't be long before Colt knew she was with Lucas at the café. Hopefully she would make it home before Fannie started spreading rumors.

  "I have been asking around about the day your grandfather passed. You told me Colt was in town that afternoon and didn't get home until after midnight."

  "Yes. Why?"

"According to some people around town Colt headed back to the farm early in the evening. That would have put him home long before your grandfather turned in for the night."

"Ok. So if he left town early evening. So what?"

"You said there was no one else around who had access to your grandfather except you. That's not true. Colt was there. If someone did switch your grandfather's insulin and it wasn't you then that only leaves..."

"Colt." Cassy couldn't believe what she was hearing. "Why would he switch Grandfather's insulin?"

"I don't know. But we can keep digging."

"I don't think we have to." Cassy just remembered how funny Colt acted when she showed him the notebook her grandfather was looking at. "Are you off for the afternoon? I would like you to come with me somewhere. I want you to be there as a witness."

"Sure. First, let's eat something for lunch, I'm starving. Then we can go."

"Ok." Cassy agreed but she knew she wasn't going to be able to eat much. Hearing what she just heard from Lucas made her sick to her stomach. Why did Colt lie to her? She motioned for Fannie to come take their order.

"So are you two ready to order?" Fannie asked.

"Yes, we are. Would you bring us both one of your delicious cheeseburgers and a coke?" Cassy asked. "Also could you make it a rush order Fannie? I have a doctor's appointment and Lucas has to get back to work."

"Sure, hon. Whatever you want. I'll get them right out."

Cassy tried to smile as Fannie headed for the kitchen. The sooner they got out of there, the better she would feel.

****

Lucas jumped in the passenger side of the truck as Cassy started the engine. "Where are we going?"
"To the Thompson's."
"Why are you going there? I really hate looking at that house." Lucas laughed. "What a waste of good money."
"I'm not sure, but there is something I need to ask Mr. Thompson and I want you to be my witness."
The rest of the ride was in silence. Cassy had to clear her head before she talked to Mr. Thompson or she could screw this up totally. She understood now why her grandfather was going through the notebook in his desk after they had returned that day. He was checking up on Colt. The feeling of panic filled up her entire body.
Cassy pulled into the drive way of the Thompson house. She opened the door and climbed out of the car with Lucas right behind her.
"Cassy wait."
Lucas was out of breath as he tried to catch up to her.
"Are you coming or not Lucas?" Cassy kept going.
"I guess I'm coming."
Cassy was met at the door by Mr. Thompson.
"Cassandra Conner. I didn't expect you to be back so soon. How are you doing since your grandfather's passing?"

"I'm doing all right. I need to ask you a question, Mr. Thompson."

"Sure Cassandra. What is it?"

"Remember the day my grandfather and I stopped by and you two were talking about the stud service you paid for?" Cassy asked.

"Sure. I remember."

"How much did you say you paid for the service?"

"Two thousand."

"And you only used my grandfather's service once, correct?"

"Only once." Gus Thompson looked confused. "What's going on Cassy?"

"I'm not sure but thank you Mr. Thompson. You've been a lot of help." Cassy climbed back into the truck and started the engine. Lucas barely made it in the truck before she took off.

"Why are you in such a hurry?" Lucas was almost out of breath trying to keep up with her.

"I think I know what happened. When Grandfather and I stopped at the Thompson's that day, Mr. Thompson made the comment about the stud fee. When we got home Grandfather checked the notebooks in his desk. After he went to sleep I took a look at the notebooks but I didn't put two and two together. Now I know what I'm looking for."

"What?" Lucas asked.

"I have to make sure before I say. I'll take you back to your car and you can either meet me back at the ranch or not."

"Why don't we just go to the ranch together now?" Lucas asked.

"I don't want Colt to get suspicious yet. If you come home with me now he'll know I lied to him. It will blow everything. I'm already risking it with

Fannie seeing us together at the café." Cassy didn't want to take the time to make Lucas understand.

"I don't know what you are talking about but I'll trust you." Lucas replied.

"I'll let you know if I need you to do anything but right now I have to do this by myself." Cassy explained. She couldn't wait to get back to the ranch and Colt.

****

Cassy parked the truck next to the house. As she climbed out, she looked to see if Colt was in the barn. Not seeing him anywhere. She headed inside the house.

"So how did the Doctor's appointment go?"

Cassy saw Colt standing in the kitchen as she walked in the backdoor.

"I guess fine. I really hate that type of appointment but there's not much I can do. I have to go." Cassy hoped he didn't catch the surprised look on her face.

"So everything checked out all right?" Colt laughed moving his fingers to make quotation marks in the air.

"Funny." Cassy smiled. "I think everything checked out fine. Thanks for asking."

"Good. I thought we could have steaks for dinner tonight, maybe a salad and some fresh ears of corn."

"That sounds great. Would you mind if I took a quick bath first and then I'll come back down and help you?" Cassy asked.

"You have plenty of time. Go ahead. I've got to go check the herd. I'll be back soon." Colt took his hat off the back of the chair and walked out the door.

"Calm down. You're going to make him suspicious if you keep acting so nervous." Cassy knew she had to keep her cool if she was going to get Colt to give her the information she needed. She grabbed her purse, the notebooks from her grandfather's desk and headed upstairs.

After she dried off, Cassy slipped on a pair of capri slacks and a sleeveless blouse and headed downstairs. She placed the notebooks back in the desk where she found them. She thought she heard Colt come back in the house.

"Colt?" She yelled as she walked towards the kitchen.

"Hi." He walked over and gave her a kiss on the cheek. "How was your bath?"

"It was refreshing. How was the herd?"

"They were all present and accounted for. I shucked the ears of corn and put them in some water on the stove. The steaks are seasoned on the platter. If you want to make the salad I'll go start the grill."

"That works for me. I'll come out and keep you company while the steaks cook."

"Bring me another beer when you come would you? It's a hot one out there tonight." Colt opened the beer he was holding, grabbed the steaks off the counter and headed outside.

Cassy took the lettuce, cucumber and tomatoes out of the refrigerator and started preparing the salad. When she finished, she put the bowl in the refrigerator, grabbed two cold beers and joined Colt outside.

"They smell great. How much longer?" Cassy asked as she opened one of the beers and handed it to Colt. "It is hot out here tonight." She opened the other beer and took a sip.

"They should be ready in about five minutes. I hope you're hungry."

"I am. I didn't get a chance to eat much lunch while I was in town because of my appointment." Cassy felt horrible making up stories but she couldn't tell him she didn't eat much at lunch because her stomach became upset when she learned he had been lying to her all along.

"Good. So which Doctor did you go see? Ole Doctor Smith? I bet he loves having beautiful young women like you come in for their appointments."

"No. I didn't see Dr. Smith." Cassy quickly tried to think of something to say not to give herself away. "I don't remember the Doctor's name. He was one of the newer Doctor's in town." Cassy hoped she covered well enough Colt wouldn't ask her anymore questions. It was her night to find out information not his.

13

"Dinner was good. Thank you." Cassy replied as she cleared the table of most of the dirty dishes.

"You're welcome. Let me help you." Colt picked up the rest of the dishes on the table and carried them to the sink. "Why don't you let me take care of those?"

"Are you sure? I don't mind washing the dishes since you cooked dinner."

"How about if I wash and you dry?" Colt smiled moving her over away from the sink.

"That sounds fair." Cassy picked up the dish towel and leaned against the cabinet watching Colt as he ran water in the sink and added the dish soap.

"I think if I still live here when I start a family I'm going to have to remodel the kitchen and put in a dishwasher."

"You mean give up all the fun of hand washing the dishes? That's just crazy talk." Colt smiled sending a now familiar chill down Cassy's body all the way to her toes.

"It might be crazy talk to you but not me. I can't believe my grandmother lived all these years without some of the modern conveniences we all take for granted."

"I guess she was happy with what she had." Colt replied.

"I believe she was. I don't remember my grandmother ever being unhappy. All my memories of her are good ones. She was always smiling or laughing." Memories of her grandmother always made Cassy smile. She could feel the love flowing through her body like she did when her grandmother would give her a huge hug. How she missed those hugs.

"So you want a family huh?" Colt asked.

"Yes, some day. Don't you?"

"I guess so. I haven't really thought about it. It wouldn't be bad having a little Colt running around."

Cassy couldn't let the twinkle she saw in the corner of his eye make her forget what she really needed to know. She needed to find out if he was in town the night her grandfather died or if he came back early like Lucas said.

"You know if you do find a woman and settle down she probably isn't going to like you going into town and staying out most of the night like you did the other night." Cassy hoped heading down this line of conversation would give her the chance to find out more information.

"I think that's probably the reason I haven't settle down or given much thought to kids. I'm still having a good time and I'm not ready to give that up."

"So what do you find to do in town? I never could figure that out. This is such a small town there can't be much to keep you busy after ten o'clock." Cassy took a plate from Colt he had washed and rinsed. She took her time drying off the water and then putting it down on the cabinet as she waited for Colt to answer her question.

"I usually have dinner and a few cups of coffee at the café and then head down to the tavern to shoot some pool and catch up with all the guys. By that time it's after midnight and then the drive back makes it an early morning."

"So is that pretty much what you did the other night when you were in town?"

"Yep. I usually don't change my routine up much."

"So that's why you woke me that night. You were just getting home from town." Cassy waited for him to answer because this was his chance to tell her the truth or lie."

"I'm sorry about waking you up. That's right. I was just getting back to the ranch and I remembered your supplies. Why are you asking me so many questions?"

He couldn't even look at her. Cassy watched his expression and he didn't even skip a beat or change his expression at all. He was good. Good at telling lies.

"No reason." Cassy paused for a minute. "You promised me a raincheck for a night of dancing. I just wondered what I was getting myself into."

****

After drying the dishes, Cassy put them away in the cabinet. There wasn't much said between the two of them after Colt lied without even blinking an eye. She wasn't sure what to do now. This was going to be a problem which required some thought. She felt Colt's arms slip around her waist.

"How about if we go upstairs?" He whispered in her ear.

"You know what Colt, after my Doctor appointment today, it's not a good night. I'm going to take some aspirin and go to bed. How about another rain check?" Cassy laid the dishtowel down on the cabinet.

"Are you sure?"

Cassy turned around and looked in his eyes knowing she was about to tell the biggest lie ever. "Positive."

"I was looking forward to us spending some time together tonight."

He was making it extremely difficult to say no. His eyes were burning holes of desire straight through to her soul. She could see the disappointment showing on his face.

"I guess I can wait a little longer." The frustration rang in his voice.

"It will do you good to wait. It will make everything that much more special." Cassy smiled as Colt pulled her closer and kissed her. It didn't feel the same as it did yesterday. If it was possible, it was more intense. Pleasure was surging through every part of her body. His kisses took her breath away. It was more than just a kiss. It was finding extreme pleasure in a kiss from the lips of someone she didn't know if she could trust. Cassy was going to have to find out soon if he had something to do with her grandfather's death.

****

"Detective Sloan, please." Cassy twirled the business card in her hand as she waited for him to come to the phone. *I hope I'm doing the right thing.*

"This is Detective Sloan. How can I help you?"

"This is Cassy Conner. I was wondering if I could talk to you."

"Sure Ms. Conner. What can I do for you?"

"I'd really like to talk in person. Would it be possible for you to make a trip out to the farm?"

"I think we could manage that Ms. Conner. How about this afternoon? Say around two."

"I'll be here. Thank you Detective Sloan." Cassy ended the phone call.

The sooner we get this over with the better. I wonder what Colt is going to do when Detective Sloan shows up again? I guess we wait and see.

****

Cassy was standing by the front door when the Detective's car pulled in the driveway. She waited for them to walk up to the door before she opened it to let both Detectives in.

"Detective Sloan. Detective Roberts. Thank you both for coming out."

"Ms. Conner. You sounded like it was important so let's sit down and you tell me what you think I need to know."

Cassy sat down in the chair as the Detectives took a seat on the couch.

"What I wanted to talk to you about was some information I found out this week. I know you are investigating what happened to my grandfather and I think the information I have will help you out." Cassy was having a hard time sitting still. She wanted this to be over.

"Why don't you take your time and tell us what this information is Ms. Conner?"

"The last time you were here I called Lucas Harding after you left. I needed to talk to someone about what we had discussed and Lucas was the perfect person. He knew my grandfather's illness well because he was one of the paramedics to answer the calls when he had problems."

"Was Mr. Harding helpful when you talked to him?" Detective Rogers asked.

"Yes. He explained to me what you meant by my grandfather having too much insulin in his blood stream and how that could have happened. We came to the same conclusion you had and that was his insulin had to have been switched."

"Is this the information you have to share with me Ms. Conner? If so you're wasting my time repeating what I told you."

"No, Detective Sloan. I apologize for not getting to the point sooner. The information I have to share with you is if you remember when I told you Colt Matthews had left for town late in the afternoon and didn't get back until early morning?"

"Yes, I do."

"Well, Lucas was talking to some people in town and he found out Colt wasn't in town all night. He had left town early in the evening and had plenty of time to make it back to the farm. Colt was familiar with my grandfather's illness. He knew about the insulin but the most important piece of information is remember me telling you I saw my grandfather going through his books at the desk? Well, I checked with Mr. Thompson again asking him what he paid for the artificial insemination fee he was charged for my grandfather's prize bull. Mr. Thompson said he paid two thousand dollars for the fee. My grandfather's books show he only charged Mr. Thompson one thousand for the fee. Here look at this."

Cassy picked the notebook up off the table where she had placed it and handed it to Detective Sloan.

"These are the notebooks my grandfather kept his records of customers, when they purchased, how much he charged and if the insemination took."

"This is all well and good Ms. Conner but I don't understand what you are getting at."

"I'm trying to tell you I think Colt Matthews was skimming from my grandfather by increasing artificial insemination fees to his customers and keeping the extra money to himself." Cassy paused for a minute shaking her head. "I even showed him the notebooks and told him Grandfather was looking through them when we returned from the Thompson's."

"That's a pretty big accusation Ms. Conner. Are you sure about that?"

"You can check the bank deposits and ask my grandfather's customers. I'll be happy to give you a list of customers and what they paid."

"And if we find out Colt Matthews was skimming money like you think, then what?"

"What do you mean then what?" Cassy asked. "Colt might have been trying to hide this information. He might have switched my grandfather's insulin. He could be the reason my grandfather is dead. I don't want to believe it but I need to know."

"I tell you what Ms. Conner, we'll do some asking around and see if the information you have given us is correct and we'll let you know what we find."

Cassy stood up with the Detectives and walked with them to the door.

"I'll be waiting to hear from one of you. Please let me know what you find out."

"We will Ms. Conner. I would suggest you don't say anything to Colt Matthews about what you told us."

"Sure. Do you think I'm in danger staying here with Colt in the bunkhouse?" Cassy asked.

"Do you have someone who can stay with you?"

"No. No one I can think of right now."

"My suggestion would be to not say anything to Mr. Matthews about our conversation. We'll check out what you told us as soon as we can." Detectives Sloan and Rogers stepped out the front door and headed for their car. "Thank you for your time Ms. Conner."

Cassy watched as they drove off. "What now?"

"Who was that?" Colt yelled as he walked in the back door.

"You mean driving off?" Cassy asked.

"Yeah. It looked like those Detectives that were here a few days ago."

Cassy watched as he took his hat off and hung it on the back of the chair. He ran his fingers through his hair and it fell perfectly back into place. He was so gorgeous. What she was thinking couldn't be true. How could he have hurt her grandfather?

"It was. Detectives Sloan and Rogers."

"What were they doing here again?" Colt asked.

"They were updating me on the findings of the Corner autopsy. They don't know for sure what happened to Grandfather so they are calling the case an accident. They are saying Grandfather took the wrong insulin by mistake and they might be closing the case."

"How does that make you feel?" Colt asked.

"I'm not sure. I guess it's good to know there isn't someone out there who could do that kind of thing and get away with it." Cassy started walking towards the kitchen. "I'm going to make some soup and a sandwich for dinner. Would you like something?"

"How about you?" Colt put his arms out and pulled her to him as she tried to pass by.

"You know Colt, it seems like I'm always telling you no." Cassy couldn't help but wonder how this man who made her body burn with desire could be guilty of killing her grandfather. "I'm sorry, but talking about my grandfather's death brings back a lot of unhappy memories. It's just not a good time."

"Ok, then how about a sandwich and some soup?" Colt reached up and took two bowls and plates out of the cabinets.

"Sounds good. Thank you for understanding."

"You know, I would never expect you to do anything you weren't ready for." Colt pulled her close. "I cared about your grandfather and I care about you. I would never do anything to hurt you."

Casey buried her head in Colt's chest. She felt so safe in his arms. She wanted everything to be all right. It had to be all right. How could she ever believe he could do something so awful?

They both ate their dinner in silence. Cassy couldn't get past the fact Colt had lied to her about the night her grandfather died. Her head was telling her she couldn't trust him and she should be afraid of what he could do, but her body and heart were telling her to keep an open mind until the truth was found out. If he was going to do anything to her, he had more than had his chance. Nothing is ever as it seems. She wasn't sure whether to listen to her head or her heart.

****

Colt was glad he got up early to do his daily inspection of the farm. It was going to be a miserably hot day. He took the saddle off the horse and led her to the stall. He threw the saddle over the railing and headed back to brush down the horse.

"Colt Matthews?" Detectives Sloan and Rogers appeared in the doorway of the barn.

"Yes. I'm Colt Matthews."

"I'm Detective Sloan and this is Detective Rogers."

He flipped open the wallet which contained his badge giving Colt a chance to look closely.

"We would like you to come down to the station with us. We would like to ask you a few questions."

"About what?" Colt asked.

"About the night James Conner was murdered."

"Murdered? " Colt didn't understand what he was saying. "Cassy told me you were thinking of closing the case and ruling it an accident."

"Well, in light of some new evidence we are keeping it open." Detective Sloan replied. "As I said before, we would like you to come with us so we can ask you some questions.

"You have to take me down to the station for that? I can tell you what you want to know right here and then you can be on your way."

"You see, Mr. Matthews, we also want to talk to you about how you skimmed money from James Conner."

"What are you talking about?" Colt asked. "I haven't skimmed money from anyone."

"If you come peacefully we won't use handcuffs, but if you resist we'll change the rules." Detective Sloan stood on one side of Colt and Detective Rogers on the other. They walked him slowly towards their squad car, each one keeping a grip on Colt's arms. Opening the door, they placed him in the back seat.

All Colt could think right now was Cassy. She didn't know where he was going and he probably wouldn't get a chance to tell her. What if they arrested him and threw him in jail?

"How am I going to explain this to her?"

****

Cassy watched as the Detectives drove out the driveway with Colt in the backseat. She was sure Colt was asking for her as they drove away.

"What have I done?"

Cassy sat down at the kitchen table and cried, not sure what she was feeling. Her emotions were jumbled. She missed her grandfather horribly. If someone helped him die, she wanted that person to pay but she didn't want it to be Colt. All the evidence they had pointed to him, but she didn't want to believe it. It couldn't be Colt. She was sure she could feel her heart breaking.

14

"We understand you were in town the night James Conner died. Is that correct?" Detective Sloan asked.

"Yes it's correct." Colt replied.

"Can you tell us exactly what you did that night? Why you were in town."

"Sure. I went into town to get some supplies. I needed a part for the tractor and I had a list and some money from Cassy. I ate dinner at the café and a few cups of coffee then I headed for the tavern to play a few games of pool."

"What did you do after that? Surely what you have told us wouldn't have taken you all night. We understand you didn't make it home until early the next morning."

"I don't know what you've heard." Colt paused for a minute trying to be careful not to give them any information they could twist around on him.

"So why don't you tell us the truth so we know exactly what happened that night." Detective Sloan asked.

"I had a few beers at the tavern while I was playing pool. I started not feeling good so I decided to head for home."

"What time was that?" Detective Rogers asked.

"It was around ten thirty but I didn't make it all the way back to the farm."

"Why not?

"I had to pull my truck over about half way home because I started feeling dizzy. I got out of the truck and threw up. I climbed back in the truck to head the rest of the way home. I don't remember anything else. I must have passed out in the truck."

"Sounds like you had more than a few beers."

"I swear I only had a few beers. They have never affected me like that before. I wasn't sure what to think. When I came to, I drove to the farm and remembered I had supplies for Cassy so I took them in the house. I put them on the kitchen cabinet and headed for the bunkhouse to get some sleep

"So did you still feel sick when you woke up the next morning?" Detective Sloan questioned.

"Not really. I remember feeling a little weak and having a hard time focusing, but it went away after I showered and had a cup of coffee."

"So who did you drink beer and play pool with that night?"

"Let's see. I remember a couple of farmhands from the Thompson farm. I played a game of pool with one of them. Oh, and Lucas Harding. He and I played a game and he bought a pitcher while we played." Colt thought back to that night and couldn't remember anyone else. "That was about it. It was shortly after that I started feeling funny and headed home."

"Lucas Harding's name seems to pop up a lot." Detective Sloan replied.

"It's a small town. It's not surprising. In his line of work he knows a lot of people."

"We did some checking, Mr. Matthews, and found out what you have been doing with the fees the Conner Farm has been receiving for services associated with prize bulls."

"What are you talking about?" Colt asked.

"We got a warrant to search through your bank records and we learned you were splitting off some of the fee and putting that money into a separate bank account."

Taking off his cowboy hat, Colt ran his fingers through his hair and put his hat back on his head.

"So you know about the money. Just who told you about the money?" Colt was positive he knew exactly who that person was. He also knew he had to be very careful what he admitted to. "I think I would like to consult my lawyer before I answer any more questions." He could only hope Bo Perkins was available.

****

"Bo, It's Colt." He paused for a minute. "I need your help."

"Sure, Colt. What can I do?"

"I need you to come bail me out of jail." Colt tried to remain calm and hold back his true feelings of anger and frustration.

"What? Why? What on earth have you done?"

"Nothing." Colt snapped. "It's a long story Bo. Just get all my paperwork together and get down here right away. Make sure you bring the file you have on the Conner farm."

"Sure. I'll be right there. I'd say don't go anywhere but I don't have to worry about that."

"Funny, Perkins. One more thing, call Chad Thompson and tell him I'm calling in my favor. I need him to take care of the Conner farm until I can get out of here. He knows what to do."

"You got it Colt. Anything else?"

"Just hurry." Colt hung up the phone. "Okay, I'm ready." He stood up from the chair and waited for the officer to escort him to his cell.

"Back in Colt. I'll let you know when you lawyer gets here."

Colt sat down on the cot in the cell. "Let's hope he hurries."

****

"So what you're trying to tell me Mr. Matthews is you used your money to keep the Conner farm afloat until James Conner got well and back on his feet. The money you added to the prize bull stud fees above what James Conner wanted to charge was a way for you to make back the money you invested in the farm. Does that sound about right?" Detective Sloan asked.

"My client has provided you with all the information you need to prove his innocence." Bo Perkins replied. "I don't believe there is anything else you need or any reason why you don't release him."

"The Judge isn't available to set bail and we need a chance to go over all the evidence you have presented to us." Detective Sloan shifted through the stack of papers. "I'm afraid until the judge is available to set bail or we can verify this information your client is going to have to be a guest of ours."

"You mean to tell me I have to stay here?" Heat flowed through his body as Colt felt the frustration building stronger. "Bo, can't you do something. I've got responsibilities at the farm. Cassy is there by herself. Chad can only help so much. He has his own farm to tend to."

"Why don't you make her a list of what she needs to take care of and we'll get it to her." Detective Sloan suggested.

"That's big of you." Colt laughed. "Why don't you let me go so I can show her?"

"Sorry Colt. It's not happening."

"I gave it a shot. Cassy can't say I didn't try."

****

"You have a visitor Mr. Matthews." The deputy unlocked the cell door.

"Who is it?"

"Follow me." Colt followed the deputy to a room with windows, a metal table and a few chairs. He stepped inside the room and sat down.

"I'll go get your guest." The deputy stepped out the door and disappeared down the hallway.

When he reappeared Cassy was with him. He unlocked the door and let her walk inside the room.

"Colt."

"What are you doing here Cassy?" It was hard for him to look her in the eyes. She was the reason he was here. He should be mad as hell at her but when she put her arms around him to hug him, those thoughts disappeared. She felt good. The deputy seemed to enjoying himself until he broke them up.

"No touching." The deputy replied.

"Sorry." Cassy smiled. "Mr. Perkins came by and paid me a visit."

Colt watched as she sat down in the chair next to him.

"He told me everything. I can't believe what you did for my grandfather. What you did for my family."

"I didn't do anything anyone else wouldn't have done." Colt replied.

"Yes you did."

Colt could hear Cassy's voice breaking.

"You did a lot. I don't know how I'm going to repay you. I feel so awful you are in here because of me. I should have talked to you first."

"I wanted to talk to you and your grandfather about this mess. I wanted to be the one to tell you." Colt could see tears welling up and begin to fall from Cassy's eyes. He reached up and wiped them away until he heard the deputy clear his throat.

"Got it. No touching."

He wanted to kiss her and tell her how he felt but he knew it wasn't allowed or the right time. He had never met another woman who grabbed his heart like she had. There was nothing he could do about it. The first day he saw Cassy Conner he knew he was in trouble.

"You don't have to repay me. I was only trying to help your grandfather. He had just lost his wife. Their son, your father, was dead and you were the only family. He didn't want me to call you because he wanted you to live your life and not be tied down to the farm. With everything he was going through, I couldn't tell him the farm was in financial trouble. Not on top of everything else."

"So you kept him liquid with your own money until things turned around?" Cassy asked.

"Yeah. I did."

"Colt, that's a lot more than anyone would have done. I can't believe you're sitting here in jail because you were being an angel in disguise. I'm so sorry things have turned out this way. I promise I'll sell the farm if I have to and get you your money back."

"You're not selling the farm." Colt exclaimed. "I won't let you do that, not even to pay me back."

"Colt I don't have the money to pay you back. The only way I would be able to get it would be to sell the farm."

"I don't want you to pay me back. Not right now. We'll work it out. Over time I'll get my money back. If we agree to keep the fees at the price I was charging, I'll be paid back in less than five years."

"I would be willing to do that, if you are willing to wait that long to be repaid."

"I'd be willing to wait forever to be repaid if it meant I could stay on the farm with you."

"Colt."

"I mean it Cassy. You drive me crazy. All I can think about is you." Colt could see the surprise in her eyes.

"We need to get you out of here. We have things to take care of back at the farm."

Cassy smiled and Colt thought for sure he could feel his heart melt in his chest.

15

All Colt could think about was how he couldn't spend another night in this jail cell. Even if he did spend it dreaming of Cassy he wanted out of here. He wanted to be back at the ranch where he could hold her in his arms and feel her bare skin next to his.

"Time to go."

Colt's thoughts were interrupted by the deputy unlocking the cell door.

"What's going on?" Colt asked.

"The charges have been dropped. You're free to go." He held the door open waiting for Colt to walk through.

"I hope you're serious because this is a sick joke if you're not." Colt hurried through the open door.

"We just need to process you and you can leave. Follow me this way." Colt walked behind the Deputy. He couldn't believe he would be back at the farm and with Cassy soon.

"Here's everything you had on you when we checked you in. Make sure you go through it and you have everything."

Colt dumped the envelope out on the counter.

"It looks like it's all here. Now get me the hell out of here."

"We're almost done. You need to sign for your belongings and we'll be done."

"I wish I could say this has been a pleasure." Colt replied as he signed the piece of paper, picked up all his belongings off the counter and put them in his pocket. He walked through the door to the lobby.

"Can I give you a ride home?" Cassy's voice surprised him.

Colt knew this was too good to be true. He was going home and Cassy Conner was going with him.

"I'd love a ride. I can't wait to get home." Colt put his arm around her waist and headed for the door. He wanted to make sure he wasn't dreaming and he wasn't going to give anyone a chance to wake him before he got what he wanted.

****

Pulling up to the house Colt jumped out of the truck not giving Cassy an opportunity to even put the truck in park. He ran around to the driver's side of the truck and waited for her to climb out.

"Why are you in such a hurry?" Cassy asked.

"If you had just spent the past two days in jail I'd like to see how excited you would be to finally be home." Colt picked Cassy up and spun her around in a circle. "I've been thinking about nothing but you." He kissed her lightly. "First things first. I want to take a shower."

"Why don't you do that? I'll fix us a sandwich and some iced tea. I'll meet you in the kitchen."

"You've got a deal lady." Colt took off running for the bunkhouse. "I promise I'll smell a lot better when I get done. Don't go anywhere."

"I'll be right here when you get back." Cassy laughed.

Colt couldn't believe what was happening. His life was turning around in circles so fast he was dizzy. His mother had always told him he would know when he met the right woman to just give fate a chance. Right now he was glad he listened.

****

Cassy finished making each of them a sandwich, filled two glasses with iced tea then put them down on the table next to the plates. She walked over to the back door waiting for Colt to come out of the bunkhouse. Watching as Colt came walking toward the house, his shirt unbuttoned, the tale blowing as the warm breeze caressed his body, his exposed chest glistened from the sun shining on his skin. She couldn't keep her eyes from noticing the beads of water flowing down a pleasure trail begging to be followed. Cassy couldn't wait until he got within her reach. She wanted to feel him not only next to her but inside of her. She wanted to drink him in, every inch.

"I've been waiting." Cassy smiled as he opened the door.

"I've been waiting a long time for you." Colt pulled her close and kissed her hard and deep.

She wasn't letting him go.

"I made you a sandwich." Cassy managed to get a few words out after catching her breath. "I don't know about you but I think I can wait to eat mine."

"Me too."

There was that smile that took her breath away.

Cassy took Colt's hands leading him up the stairs to her bedroom. She ran her hands over his chest, her fingers delicately combing the tufts of hair, kissing his skin as she took in the scent of him. His shirt fell to the floor. She made her way down his chest, unbuckled his belt and unzipped his jeans. She wanted him now and from the bulge in his jeans, Cassy knew he felt the same. She helped him with the buttons on her blouse and shorts. Colt managed to quickly unfasten her bra and leave it and her panties lying in a pile on the bedroom floor.

She wanted to take everything slow and enjoy every inch of each other but she couldn't fight the desire rushing through her body and have him inside of her.

Colt laid her gently on the bed lying on top of her kissing her neck and down her chest. He caressed each of her breasts, cupping them in his hands and massaging them as he ran his tongue gently around each nipple. They responded to his touch, becoming hardened beads, the excitement making her body flame.

Cassy arched with each moment of pleasure, pressing her moist, wet sex against his erection, making him harder. She gasped as he made his way between her legs, his tongue caressing her until she couldn't and didn't want to stop the feeling of pleasure rushing through her body. She ran her fingers through his hair as he made her moan with ecstasy. She wanted more. She wanted him inside her.

Colt began kissing her abdomen, moving his way back up her body until he found her breasts, hard and aching for him. She placed her hands on his hips and pulled him up where she could feel the end of his penis pressing firm against her. Moving her hips against him she gave him complete access to her. She felt him enter her slowly then he pulled back out slowly as if he was teasing her senses. Each tender motion sent her body to the edge of pleasure. Their bodies moved in perfect rhythm until they both reached a moment of ecstasy. Cassy's moans of pleasure begging Colt not to stop didn't fall on deaf ears. He kept pleasing her as she felt another wave come over her body. He didn't deny her anything.

They both collapsed in exhaustion trying to catch their breath. Nothing was said. There were no words to follow what just happened. They had just told the other what they felt.

****

Cassy woke to darkness outside and an empty bed. She picked up her bathrobe and headed downstairs. There was a wonderful fragrance coming from the kitchen. If she wasn't mistaken, she thought she heard someone singing along to the radio. Walking into the kitchen she caught a glimpse of Colt busy by the stove.

"You have a nice voice and something smells wonderful."

"Well, look who's awake." Colt replied.

"What are you making?" She walked up behind Colt sliding her arms around his waist.

"I'm making you some bacon and eggs. I thought you might be hungry."

"I'm starving." Cassy took two glasses out of the cabinet and poured each of them a glass of milk. "How long have you been awake?"

"For about an hour." Colt replied. "I watched you sleep for a little while then I slipped out of bed to come make us something to eat. I hope you don't mind but I tossed the sandwiches you made earlier. I didn't think it would be a good idea to eat them."

"Thank you. I had forgotten about them." Cassy smiled as Colt pulled her close to him.

"I think we forgot about everything but each other for a little while. How about if we go back up and pick up where we left off?"

"What and throw away this wonderful meal you just made? It would be a shame."

"It would be a shame but it would be a lot of fun." Colt continued to kiss her neck.

"I'm sure it would be fun but I'm starving and this looks wonderful."

Cassy sat down at the table smiling as Colt placed a plate of food in front of her kissing her lightly on the lips before she took a bite.

"I love you Cassy Conner."

Taken by surprise Cassy couldn't say a word. She watched the most gorgeous cowboy butt walk away from her and back to the stove. "That cowboy butt is all mine." She whispered to herself smiling.

****

They both devoured the food on their plate.

"That was perfect." Cassy said. "Thank you." She picked up the dishes off the table and took them to the sink.

"So what's on the agenda for the rest of the evening?" Cassy asked as she felt Colt walk up behind her and slide his arms around her waist.

"I was thinking maybe we could spend it in bed."

Cassy leaned back against his body. The warmth of his skin against hers brought back memories. She was having a hard time concentrating on anything but him.

"What do you say?"

His moist kisses against her neck made her weak. She turned facing him and slid her arm around his neck. "Yes."

She felt him sweep her up in his arms and head for the stairs. Just as they passed the table the doorbell rang.

"Who in the hell could that be?" Colt stopped.

"I have no clue. If you put me down, I'll go check." Cassy laughed.

"I say we just pretend we didn't hear it and keep going upstairs."

The doorbell rang again.

"They're not going away." Cassy replied. "Put me down and I'll see if I can get rid of them."

Cassy straightened her hair and bathrobe and went to answer the door.

"Cassy Conner?"

The young delivery man asked as she opened the door.

"Yes."

"I have a certified letter for you."

He handed Cassy a clipboard with an envelope attached.

"Would you please sign?"

Cassy signed on the line and handed him back the clipboard. She watched as he tore off the return card and handed Cassy the envelope.

"Have a nice day."

Looking at the return address on the envelope, Cassy read it was from a lawyer's office.

"Who was it?" Colt asked.

"It was a delivery man with a certified letter. It's from some lawyer."

"Are you going to open it and see what it is?" Colt asked.

"Of course." Cassy slipped her finger under the edge of the envelope and opened the seal. Taking the letter out, she began reading. "You're not going to believe this."

"What?" Colt moved closer to her trying to read what was written on the paper.

"I guess I have a brother." Cassy laughed. "According to this letter Lucas Harding is my half-brother and he wants his share of the Conner farm."

****

Cassy poured a cup of coffee as Colt sat at the table looking through the papers.

"Wow, this is crazy. Did you have any idea?" Colt asked.

"No, I had no clue." Cassy sat down in the chair next to Colt.

"Your father was a busy man. Lucas is probably a few years older than you so that means you father was messing around with Lucas' mother around the time he married your mother."

"I really don't want to think about that part. What it means is my father wasn't the person I thought he was and neither is Lucas." Cassy replied.

"So your grandfather's will left me half and you half of the Conner farm so that tells us he had no idea he had a grandson."

"So if my grandfather had no clue Lucas Harding was his grandson then how did Lucas get the sample to do a DNA test?" Cassy asked.

"That's a good question. I would assume he didn't get it with your grandfather's permission."

"Correct. I know one thing for sure and that is I'm going to have my own testing done to make sure this information is correct." Cassy replied. "I'm not going to just hand over part the farm my grandfather worked all of his life to build. The farm you sunk your money in to keep running. He must think I'm crazy if he thinks I'm just going to roll over."

"That's the woman I fell in love with." Colt smiled.

Cassy moved from her chair and sat down in Colt's lap wrapping her arms around his neck.

"I love you Colt Matthews." Cassy kissed him softly on the neck. "Now where did we leave off before we were so rudely interrupted by the doorbell?"

"I do believe I remember."

Colt stood up from his chair taking Cassy with him in his arms. "I believe right here."

Cassy held on while Colt carried her carefully up the stairs to her bedroom and laid her gently on the bed.

"Oh yes. Now I remember." Cassy laughed as Colt began undressing her.

16

"Lucas. Hi, it's Cassy Conner."

"Cassy."

"Or, from what you're trying to pull, should I say Brother?" Cassy sat down on the edge of her bed putting his business card back in the drawer of her nightstand.

"I see you received the letter from my lawyer."

"Yes I did." Cassy snapped. "So you want me to just believe you are my brother and you want half of my family farm?"

"Now that I know for sure I am family, I just want my share of what belongs to me. Nothing more."

"You know my grandfather left half the ranch to me and half to Colt Matthews."

"Then I'll contest the will and take my third." Lucas laughed. "A half or a third, either way I get what belongs to me."

"So, Lucas, exactly what makes you think you're my half-brother? Did Grandfather say something to you to make you think you were from this family?" Cassy wanted some answers from him.

She hoped he could be honest enough to give her that much.

"No. Your grandfather never said a word and I never told him what I knew."

"And you never said anything to me either. You had to have been working on this the day I arrived on the farm and you never said a word." Cassy could tell her voice was becoming louder as her frustration grew. "All the times we were together you never said a word. Why?"

"I had to have proof. You weren't going to believe me, a perfect stranger, if I told you I was your brother."

"So who told you or gave you the idea you are a Conner?" Cassy was getting disgusted with his attitude. "I want to know the truth Lucas."

"Mother told me." He replied.

"Your Mother?" Cassy paused for a minute. She remembered Lucas telling her about his Mother and how she couldn't remember who he was most of the time.

"You told me your Mother can't even remember your name most of the time and you believed her when she told you a wild story like this?"

"I didn't believe her at first. She apologized to me for not having a man around when I was growing up. Several times she mentioned if your father hadn't run off and married someone else we could have had a nice life. After her repeating herself over and over I decided I would take her serious and find out if she was telling me the truth. On one of my emergency calls for your grandfather I took a sample swab and I had it tested. You have the results."

"You took a sample from Grandfather without his permission?" Cassy was furious. "Not that I don't trust you or your lawyer, but I want to have my own DNA testing done. I'm going to set something up and I'll let you know where and when. I'm going to be a little more considerate and respectful. I plan to give you the information you need myself instead of having my lawyer talk to your lawyer. You know how that goes don't you?"

"You sound like you aren't too happy to find out you have a brother Cassy. After all these years of being an only child you would think you would relish the fact you have some family."

Cassy could hear Lucas' laughing on the other end of the phone.

"It's the way you let me know. Like I told you earlier, you've known for how long? We've been around each other several times and you choose to tell me in a letter from your lawyer. How welcoming and thoughtful of you."

"I can see we are going to be a loving family just like I thought. You don't trust me and I don't trust you. We're already having disagreements just like families do."

"I'll let you know when and where to get the testing done. I might call you with the information or I may just have it delivered by mail. It'll be a surprise." Cassy mused.

"Not funny." Lucas replied.

"Hopefully it will be quick and we'll get this out of the way and go on with our lives."

"I'll be waiting."

Cassy ended the phone call and put her cell phone down on the nightstand.

"Who was that?" Colt asked as he walked out of the shower with a towel wrapped loosely around his waist.

"It was Lucas. I called him to let him know I wanted to set up my own testing. Not that I didn't trust him, which I don't." Cassy laughed.

"So what did he have to say about that?"

"He wasn't too happy but who cares. All he wants is part of the farm."

"You might have to give it to him you know." Colt replied. "If he is right about being your half-brother he could contest the will and ask for part of your Grandfather's inheritance."

"He can ask all he wants. Until I'm sure he is my half-brother he gets nothing from me."

"I'd hate to mess with you lady." Colt chuckled.

There was that smile, the one that sent her over the edge. The corner of his lip turned up just a little which gave him a look which was very sensuous. Cassy moved closer to him and with one pull she dropped the towel from his waist to the floor.

"Really? Are you sure?"

Colt stood his ground as Cassy worked her magic. Taking him in her hands she gently massaged until he became hard and firm. Stepping back, she dropped her nightgown on the floor then bent down on her knees. Cassy's tongue began licking, first up the shaft of his penis then down. Going back up, she placed her hand around the base of him and began circling the top with her tongue. She took him in her mouth little by little until she had all of him she could take. Cassy could hear moans coming from deep inside Colt as she took him in and out in a rhythm. She could feel his hands guiding her as she tasted him becoming more and more excited. Cassy felt Colts hands take her arms and pull her up to him.

"I want to be inside you." Colt laid her across the bed burying himself between her legs.

"Well if you put it that way." Cassy smiled knowing exactly what she was wanting from him and he didn't waste any time giving it to her

****

"Are you sure you don't want me to go into town with you?" Colt asked as he watched Cassy climb into the driver's side of the truck.

"No. I'll be all right. Thanks for volunteering though." He shut the door as she reached for the seatbelt. "Besides you've been busy with other things. There's a lot for you to catch up on around the farm."

"By other things I believe you are talking about you." Colt laughed. "Well, what can I say? You're irresistible." Colt could feel his heart flutter. He knew he was a goner. He had fallen for her with everything he had. He leaned in and gave her a kiss.

"Be careful, please. Make sure you come back."

"I will. I'll be expecting dinner on the table when I get home."

"You got it lady." Colt stepped back and watched her drive off. "Colt Matthews you're a lucky man.

****

"I'm Cassy Conner. I have an appointment with Mr. Tomlinson.

"Yes, Ms. Conner. Mr. Tomlinson is expecting you. Have a seat and I'll let him know you are here."

Cassy waited as the receptionist behind the desk dialed her phone. Not sure exactly what she needed to do, Cassy turned to Alan Tomlinson because her grandfather trusted him. He had to be a decent person. Hopefully he would keep his fees down and work quickly.

"Mr. Tomlinson will see you now Ms. Conner. Please follow me." Cassy followed the receptionist down a long hallway to a closed door. Lightly knocking, she cracked opened the door, looked in then opened the door the rest of the way. Cassy could see an older man sitting behind a big wooden desk. He stood up as she walked in the room.

"Cassandra Conner, it's nice to meet you."

Cassy shook his hand he extended as he walked around the desk.

"Your grandfather spoke a lot about you. I feel like I know you."

"It's nice to meet you, Mr. Tomlinson." Cassy sat down in a chair in front of his desk. "Call me Cassy, please."

"Of course Cassy. You mentioned you need some legal advice concerning your grandfather. By the way, I am so sorry about your loss. James Conner was a wonderful person and close friend."

"Thank you. Well, I received this letter in the mail yesterday." Cassy handed him the letter across the desk. "It's was delivered to me registered mail. As you can see it came from Lucas Harding's attorney informing me he is the illegitimate son of my father. Lucas is asking for his share of the family inheritance which means part of the Conner farm."

"I see that. So have you talked to Mr. Harding?"

"Yes. I called him to let him know I received the letter. I had some questions for him about why he thought he was a Conner and why he never mentioned anything about it until my grandfather passed."

"And his answer was…?"

"He never told my grandfather because he received the results right before his death. His mother is the person who gave him this information. Lucas took a sample swab from Grandfather on one of the emergency calls he made to the farm. It had to have been when Grandfather was not coherent."

"Why would you say that, Cassy?"

"I know my grandfather. He was a good man and a trusting soul, probably too trusting. If Lucas believed strongly enough he was a Conner, my grandfather would have never questioned him. He certainly wouldn't have asked him to take a DNA test."

"You're probably right Cassy. James was a good man and he would have welcomed Lucas with open arms. It's too bad Lucas had to go about this the wrong way."

"I agree. So now we need to find out if he is telling us the truth." Cassy replied.

"Well first thing we need to do is new testing. We aren't going to just take his word for it. The testing could have been compromised and the results would be bad. After we get those results back then we will look at what we need to do legally."

"Ok. So where do I go to do the testing?" Cassy asked.

"I'll set up the testing with the lab here at the local hospital. They will contact you and set up an appointment. It should take about three to four weeks to get the results back."

"That's a long time." Cassy replied. "I guess it's all right though. I'm not in any hurry."

"It's about standard time for test results. It will give you time to adjust to the thought you may have a half-brother."

"I guess you're right. I'm having a hard time believing it now. It might give me some time to talk to some of Father and Grandfather's friends who still live around here. Maybe I can get some information to help me put the pieces together from them."

"I'll give you a call if I need anything."

Cassy stood up from her chair and shook Alan Tomlinson's hand.

"Thank you Mr. Tomlinson. I'll wait for your call."

He walked her out the office door, down the hallway and out to the lobby area. He took a business card out of the holder on the receptionist's desk.

"Please call me if there is anything else I can do for you. Otherwise we'll talk when I get the results back."

"Thanks again Mr. Tomlinson."

Cassy walked out of the front door. The day hadn't built up its heat yet. "I wonder."

Cassy walked down to the café only a few doors down. She sat down in the booth closest to the door. It wasn't long before Fannie greeted her with a menu.

"What brings you here at this time of the day hun?"

"I had an appointment in town so I thought I would stop and have an early lunch before heading back to the farm." Cassy opened the menu and pretended to glance through.

"So how is Colt these days?' Fannie asked.

"He's doing well. I'll let him know you asked about him." Cassy smiled.

"You do that. Tell that handsome hunk he hasn't paid me a visit in a few weeks. I'm missing his lovely smile, if you know what I mean." Fannie winked at Cassy.

"Yes, I know exactly what you mean about his lovely smile." She replied. "I'll make sure he knows."

"Now what can I get you hun?"

"I'll have one of your delicious cheeseburgers and a diet soda." Cassy handed Fannie back the menu.

"Sure thing. It will be out in a few minutes."

"Thanks Fannie. By the way, how many nursing homes are here in the City?"

"There's only one. The Unity Nursing Home that's right off the highway as you head south."

"Sure." Cassy replied. "I know where you are talking about. So that's the only one? Thank you, Fannie."

"Are you planning on visiting someone there?" Fannie asked.

"No. I just remember someone mentioning a nursing home here before Grandfather passed away. I would volunteer at a nursing home when I lived in Texas. I thought I might do something like that here."

"Well, that's sweet of you dear. I'm sure those old people would love to have the company." Fannie replied. "I'll go get your order. You sit tight."

"I'll be here. Thanks for the information Fannie."

"I hope Mrs. Harding is up for company because I think I should pay her a visit." Cassy smiled knowing she would be late getting home and Colt would be worried about her but she needed to do this to settle some questions she had about her Father only Mrs. Harding could answer.

****

"Can I help you?"

"Hi." Cassy replied as she walked towards the front desk of the Unity Nursing Home. "I am interested in maybe doing some volunteer work. I wondered if that would be possible and who I need to talk to."

"How wonderful of you. Our residents love to have visits from people. Let me find our Director and you can talk to her."

Cassy looked around the room and down the hallways as she waited for the receptionist to return. She noticed several residents being wheeled around. This could be interesting. She noticed the receptionist talking to a woman in the hallway. She took the wheelchair from the woman then began pushing her towards the door. The woman smiled at Cassy as she walked towards her.

"Hi, I'm Angela Parker. I'm the director of Unity. I understand you are interested in doing some volunteer work here."

"Ms. Parker. I'm Cassy Conner." She shook her hand. "Yes, I'm interested in volunteering. I did some volunteering when I lived in Texas. I would like to do the same here if you allow it."

"We sure do. In fact, I wish more people around town would feel like you do. The residents of Unity love to have visitors." Angela smiled.

"Your receptionist said the same thing. I take it you don't have many regular visitors to Unity."

"Not really. We have a few family members who visit on a regular basis but not many other visitors. Around the holidays people feel the need to visit or we have performers come in and give shows for the residents. It depends on what our Program Director has lined up."

"An acquaintance of mine told me about you. His mother is a resident here."

"What's his name?"

"Lucas Harding. I believe his mother has Alzheimer's."

"Of course, Lucas. He visits at least once a month sometimes more. His mother has been here for over five years. Would you like to meet her?"

"Yes, I would love to. I told Lucas if I came to volunteer, I would make sure and visit his mother." Cassy smiled at Angela.

"Follow me." Cassy walked behind Angela as she headed down the long hallway to room 300."

"Sarah. Hi Sarah. It's Angela. How are you doing today? You have a visitor." The Director kept talking to her as she fluffed her pillows. "Maybe you can wake up and talk to her."

Cassy noticed Angela nod to her as if she was giving her the permission to go ahead and talk to her.

"Mrs. Harding. I'm Cassy Conner. I'm a friend of your son Lucas." Cassy sat down in the chair next to Sarah's bed.

"Lucas."

Cassy could swear she heard her whisper his name.

"Yes ma'am. Lucas." She watched Sarah's expression turn to a smile as she heard his name.

"She is in and out. As you talk to her, you will learn to tell if she is listening to you. Lucas picked it up right away. He is really good with her. He could probably give you some tips." Angela replied. "I would like to show you the rest of the nursing home. We'll see if volunteering is something you really want to do."

"Sure." Cassy stood up and walked to the door with Angela. "Goodbye Mrs. Harding. It was a pleasure to meet you."

"Lucas." Sarah whispered.

"Right down this hallway is our day room. We like to bring our residence in here to give them a different environment for a few hours a day. We have games and activities planned by our Program Director."

Cassy listened to Angela as they walked down the hallway. She couldn't get her mind off Sarah Harding. She wanted to talk to her longer, spend more time with her. She was a connection to her father. One she wasn't willing to let go of so soon.

****

Colt watched through the window as the daylight began to fade. "Where the hell is she?" He opened the back door and stepped outside. Kicking the dust around in the driveway he saw headlights in the distance.

"It's about time." He waited for Cassy to pull in the driveway and met her beside the door of the pickup. "Hey, stranger. I was worried about you."

"Hi." Cassy slid out of the pickup and hugged his neck. "I got tied up in town." She took his hand and headed for the house. "I'm starving. What's for dinner?"

"I made some spaghetti and meatballs. I didn't know what time you were going to be home, so all I need to do is make the pasta."

Colt smiled as Cassy slid her arms around his waist.

"You are the most wonderful man. I don't know how I got so lucky." Her eyes seemed to glow when she looked at him.

"I'm the lucky one." Colt pulled her close lightly touching her lips with his. He could feel her body responding to his touch. He kissed her harder as she let out a sigh.

"Are you still hungry?"

"Yes."

She laid her head on his shoulder.

"Let me make you something to eat."

"I thought you would never ask." Cassy replied.

****

"So you said you got tied up in town. What tied you up?' Colt asked

"I talked to the lawyer. He is going to set up testing time for Lucas and I to be tested and let me know." Cassy paused for a minute. "I also stopped by the Unity Nursing Home."

"Why did you stop there?" Colt asked.

"I met Sarah Harding, Lucas' mother." Cassy smiled at Colt. "I have been thinking about her ever since I got the letter from Lucas saying he was my half-brother. Since I was in town I thought I would try to meet her."

"She has Alzheimer's right? Why would you want to meet her?"

"Lucas mentioned there were some moments when she was lucid. She would remember who he was and everything."

Cassy twirled her pasta on her fork.

"I thought maybe if I met her and gained her trust she would maybe share some memories with me about my father."

"You really think she has something to tell you about your father you don't already know?" Colt asked.

"I'm not sure but it's worth a try. If what Lucas said is really true and he is my half-brother, she knew my father when he was younger. I just thought I would see how she was different from my mother."

"You really want to know that?" Colt laughed. "He married your mother not Sarah Harding. Your father might have not even known she was pregnant with Lucas or maybe she's lying about his father. After all, she doesn't remember much."

"You're right. He did marry my mother and not Sarah but there had to be something about her he liked maybe even loved?"

"I hope you don't go digging up my old girlfriends to find out about them."

"Very funny. Speaking of old girlfriends, Fannie told me you need to get your gorgeous smile into the café and see her. It's been way too long." Cassy patted him on the hand.

"Fannie. She's one of kind. If I hadn't fallen for you she was my next choice."

"That's really good to know."

Colt took Cassie's hand and pull her to him. She curled up in his lap and kissed him on the neck running her hand down his perfect chest. She knew exactly what Colt liked and how to make him give in. "So can Fannie do this?"

"I don't think so."

Cassy heard Colt sigh as she kissed his neck right where she knew he liked.

"I love you Cassy."

"I love you too Colt." Cassy kissed him gently on the lips. "Dinner was wonderful."

"Fannie taught me how to make it."

17

    Cassy pulled into a parking spot in front of the doctor's office. She was a few minutes early for her appointment but she knew there would be paperwork involved. As she walked up to the front door, Lucas came walking out.
    "Well, well. Look's who's here." Lucas grinned. "It's been awhile, Sis."
    "Lucas." Cassy waited for him to walk out the door before she started through.
    "See you around."
    Cassy kept going without saying a word.
    "He can be so arrogant." She whispered as she watched him climb in his truck and drive away.
    "Cassy Conner. I have a ten o'clock appointment."
    "Sure Ms. Conner. Would you please fill out these papers on the back and front and I'll need a copy of your insurance card, please."
    Cassy took her wallet out of her purse and handed the nurse her insurance card. The nurse took a quick photocopy and handed it back to her.

Cassy found an empty seat in the waiting area and began filling out the forms.

"Ms. Conner. The doctor will see you now." A nurse called her from a side door of the waiting area. "Follow me."

Cassy followed her back to a room where she climbed up on an exam table and waited. A tall, attractive, well dressed female doctor entered the room.

"Cassy Conner? I'm Dr. Jones. I understand you are here for some testing."

Cassy watched her sit down on a rolling stool and move close to the exam table. The nurse was by the counter putting on rubber gloves and handing the doctor a pair. She opened up a sealed paper packet and pulled out what looked to Cassy like a long Q-tip and handed it to the doctor.

"Open wide. This will only take a few seconds and we'll be done."

Cassy open her mouth as Dr. Jones rubbed the swab inside her mouth and under her tongue. The nurse opened a plastic zipper bag which she had written on the outside. Dr. Jones placed the swab in the plastic bag then zipped it closed.

"Well, that's all there is to it." Dr. Jones smiled. "We should have the results back in three to four weeks." The nurse picked up everything from the cabinet and headed out the door.

"Thank you, Dr. Jones. Will you call me with the results or will they go directly to my lawyer?" Cassy asked.

"The results will come directly from the lab and go to your lawyer."

"Great."

"Lucas is a good guy. You could do worse than to have him for a half- brother." Dr. Jones replied.

"Really? How do you know Lucas?"

"Let's just say, he's a close friend of mine. We met at the hospital."

"That makes sense. He's a paramedic and you're a doctor. Perfect match?" Cassy laughed.

"Something like that." Dr. Jones replied. "His mother is also a patient of mine."

"Lucas told me about his mother. I met her yesterday when I toured the nursing home."

"You toured Unity Nursing Home? I thought your grandfather passed."

"He did. I was thinking about volunteering there in my free time." Cassy replied.

"That would be nice. They could use some volunteers. Not many people in this town think it's important to even visit their own relatives, much less strangers. I know the residents appreciate the company. They love it when I come to visit and they're all full of stories."

"Lucas told me his mother had moments of where she remembered him. That has to be so hard for him to visit time after time and not have her remember who he is."

"I'm sure it is. It would be hard for me. It was nice to meet you Cassy. I hope everything turns out like you want it. You seem to be a nice person."

"Thanks, Dr. Jones. Good luck with Lucas. I'll put in a good word for you." Cassy climbed off the exam table, picked up her purse and headed for her car.

****

"Hi, Ms. Conner. It's good to see you again." Angela Parker came out of her office to greet Cassy. "I didn't expect you back so soon."

"I was in town for an appointment so I wanted to stop by. I don't have much time but I thought I could pay a visit to a few of the residents. Maybe take them for a walk, if that's all right with you."

"That's perfectly fine with me."

"I'd like to stop in and see Sarah Harding first." Cassy smiled.

"She would love that. You remember her room?" Angela asked.

"Yes." Cassy headed down the hallway towards room three hundred. She walked through the doorway and noticed Sarah Harding sitting up in the chair next to her bed. Cassy walked over and sat down in the empty chair next to her.

"Hi again Mrs. Harding. Do you remember me?"

Cassy didn't notice any movement from her.

"I'm a friend of your son, Lucas." Cassy added.

"Lucas." Sarah Harding whispered.

"Yes, Lucas." Cassy repeated. "I just ran into Lucas this morning."

"You saw my son? Is he here?"

"He's not here Mrs. Harding. He'll probably stop by soon. I saw him at the doctor this morning."

"Is he all right? Why was he at the doctor?"

"He's fine. Lucas is fine. He was there for a checkup that's all."

"Good. He's all right. Good."

"How are you, Mrs. Harding? Are you feeling all right?" Cassy watched the expression on her face relax.

"Yes dear. I'm fine. You look lovely today. How do you know my Lucas?"

"I met Lucas when he helped my grandfather."

"Was your grandfather sick dear?"

"Yes he was, but Lucas helped him and he was fine." Cassy smiled.

"Do you remember my grandfather, Mrs. Harding? His name was James Conner." Cassy watched her expression for any change.

"James Conner." Sarah Harding replied. "You belong to James Conner?"

"I'm his granddaughter. He passed away several weeks ago."

"Lucas told me about your grandfather passing. He told me he killed him."

Cassy gasped. She couldn't believe what she was hearing. Surely Sarah Harding didn't know what she was talking about but just in case, Cassy took her cell phone out of her purse and pushed the memo record button on the side.

"What do you mean Mrs. Harding? Why would Lucas kill my grandfather?" Casssy asked.

"Shhh." Sarah Harding placed her fingers up against her lips. "It's a secret. Lucas told me not to say anything to anyone."

"It's all right Mrs. Harding, Lucas and I are friends. You can tell me anything."

"Lucas snuck in James Conner's house and gave him a shot. Lucas said James didn't fight him. He told James he was taking care of him. It was easy Lucas said."

"Why would Lucas do something like that Mrs. Harding?"

"He wants to give me a nice home. Lucas deserves that farm. After all he was supposed to be a Conner you know. If his father would have married me instead of that other bitch, Lucas would have what he deserves. Instead, he has to get rid of that girl that lives there now and some farmhand so he can have it all. He promised me he would make a room for me when he finally got rid of everyone who doesn't belong."

"Are you sure about that Mrs. Harding? Do you remember the girl's name?"

"How could I forget? Her name sounded a lot like yours. It was Cassy."

Cassy couldn't say anything. Her heart was in her throat and beating fast. She stopped the recording on her phone, picked up her purse and backed slowly out of the room. The expression on Sarah Harding's face didn't change at all. She was talking about her son killing a man and her expression didn't change. Was she telling the truth? Cassy wanted to run. No, she needed to run. She wanted to get to Colt as fast as she could. She needed him now.

"Are you all right Cassy?" She could hear Angela Parker's voice coming from down the hallway. Cassy took a few deep breaths to keep from passing out. She had to calm down. She didn't want to tell anyone else about what Sarah Harding had said, not until she had a chance to talk to Colt.

"I'm fine Angela. I just remembered I have somewhere else I need to be. I'll have to come back again when I have more time." Cassy could feel her heart beat slowing down to a normal pace. Her breathing was becoming normal. She hoped the color had returned to her face.

"That would be great Cassy. It is so nice of you to spend some of your free time with us."

"Next time I'll try to let you know before I show up." Cassy replied. "I've really got to go." Cassy headed down the hallway to the front door.

"Cassy. Imagine running into you here?" Lucas was standing right in front of her.

"Lucas."

"What are you doing here Cassy? You don't know anyone in this nursing home."

"No, I don't. I was in town and I remembered you talking about your mother being in a nursing home. I always volunteered when I lived in Texas. I thought maybe I could do the same here at Unity." Cassy hoped he was buying everything she was saying. She felt like she was a little kid caught with her hand in the cookie jar.

"How nice of you." Lucas replied.

"By the way, Angela introduced me to your mother. She's a very nice lady."

"You talked to Mother?" Lucas asked.

"Not really. She didn't have much to say. She did seem to come alive when I mentioned your name." Cassy smiled.

"Nothing like a mother's love." Lucas replied.

"I've really got to go. I have to meet Colt back at the farm." Cassy started walking toward the front door as calmly as she could. The last thing she needed was Lucas suspecting anything. "See you around Lucas. It was nice to see you again Angela."

"You too, Cassy."

Opening the truck door Cassy slipped in the seat, took her keys out of her purse and started the truck. She couldn't wait to get home to Colt. She had to tell someone about her visit with Sarah Harding before she exploded. It's a good thing she recorded it on her cell phone or no one would believe her.

****

"Colt." Cassy slid out of the truck and slammed the door. "Colt. Where are you?" She didn't see him anywhere outside the house or barn so she headed for the house. Opening the back door she ran in looking around the kitchen and living room.

"Colt. Are you in here?" There was no answer so Cassy headed back outside. He had to be her somewhere. She saw him heading towards her from the barn.

"There you are." Cassy ran towards him.

"What's going on? Colt asked as she reached him out of breath. "Are you all right?"

"Yes. Come with me. I have something I need to you to listen to." Cassy grabbed Colt's arm and started heading towards the house.

"What's going on Cassy?" Colt stopped waiting for her to answer. "How did your appointment in town go? Is that what this is all about?"

"I'll tell you everything but let's go in the house."

"Okay. I guess."

Cassy began pulling Colt towards the house almost at a trot. They walked in the backdoor of the house and Cassy pointed to the chair at the kitchen table for Colt to sit down.

"I don't know what happened to you in town today, but from the way you're acting it must be good. I can't wait to hear this."

Cassy sat down in the chair next to Colt.

"I went to my doctor's appointment this morning and I ran into Lucas as I was going in the building. He must have just finished his appointment. Dr. Jones and I talked while she was taking care of my DNA test and I learned she was Sarah Harding's doctor."

"Sarah Harding, Lucas' mother?" Colt asked.

"Yes. Anyway, I decided I would stop by the Unity Nursing Home on my way out of town and visit with Sarah Harding again."

"So how was she today?"

"Listen for yourself?" Cassy pulled the cell phone out of her purse and played the memo recording for Colt. When it was finished she closed the cell phone and looked at the expression on Colt's face.

"What do you think?" She asked.

"So she told you Lucas was responsible for your grandfather's death so he could inherit the Conner farm. Now he's planning to do something to get me and you out of the way so he can have the whole farm and move his mother in?"

Cassy could tell by the expression on Colt's face he was just as shocked by Sarah Harding's story as she was.

"Do you think we should believe her? Lucas said she had time of lucid thinking and would remember him and her surroundings. Do you think she is telling me the truth?"

"I don't know what to say Cassy. It sounds like the rambling of an old woman who's crazy. I don't know if anyone is going to believe it."

"So do we just forget about it and go on like nothing happened?"

"Boy, I'm not sure what to do." Colt took off his hat and ran his hands through his hair. "I would be afraid to just forget about it. What if the old woman was telling the truth?"

"I'm going to call Detectives Sloan and Rogers and see what they think." Cassy stood up from the table. "I don't know about you, but Sarah Harding scared me Colt. I can't just forget about it. You should have seen the look in her eyes."

As Colt took her in his arms she could feel his heart beating almost as fast as hers. She knew he didn't like what he heard any more than she did.

****

"Detective Sloan, Detective Rogers."

Cassy smiled as the two men walked up to the front door. "Please come in." Cassy moved aside as they both walked in the living room and sat down on the couch.

"Ms. Conner. Your call sounded important. What is it we can do for you this time?" Detectives Sloan and Rogers both pulled out small notebooks and a pen from their jacket pockets.

Cassy heard Colt walk in the back door of the house. She waited for him to sit down in the chair next to her before she continued.

"You remember Colt Matthews?" Cassy asked the detectives.

"Yes, we do. Is it all right for him to hear what we have to discuss?" Detective Sloan asked.

"Yes. I want Colt here because this involves him also." Cassy replied.

"If it's fine with you, then go ahead."

"I was in town yesterday so I stopped at the Unity Nursing Home. I paid a visit to Sarah Harding."

"Sarah Harding?" Detective Sloan asked. "Isn't she Lucas Harding's mother?"

"Yes."

"Why would you go visit her?" Detective Rogers asked.

"Lucas mentioned his mother was in the Unity Nursing Home and I was interested in doing some volunteer work. When I lived in Texas I tried to volunteer as much time as I could at the local nursing homes. Anyway, I wanted to continue doing the same since I moved back here especially after losing my grandfather. This was the second visit I had with Sarah Harding."

"You'd been to visit her before?"

"Yes, once for just a short visit. This visit was different."

Cassy took her cell phone out of her pocket and played the memo recording for the two detectives. When it was finished she closed her cell phone and left it lying on the table.

"What do you think?" Cassy looked at each of the Detectives.

"So that was Sarah Harding? What made you decided to record what she was saying?" Detective Sloan asked.

"I'm not sure." Cassy replied. "It was the look on her face and when I mentioned I was a friend of Lucas. She seemed to come alive. I thought maybe she would say something I could play back to Lucas to make him feel good."

"Well, I'd say what you recorded certainly isn't something Lucas is going to be proud of." Detective Rogers laughed.

"Mr. Matthews, didn't you tell us you were playing pool with Lucas Harding the night James Conner passed?" Detective Rogers asked Colt.

"Yes. I was at the bar that night. I had a few beers and played a few games of pool after dinner."

"You said you started not feeling well so you headed back to the farm right?"

"Yes. That's right. I pulled over because I got sick and then passed out in the truck. When I woke up, I drove the rest of the way to the farm, unloaded the supplies and went to bed."

"You never told me that Colt," Cassy replied. "Why didn't you tell me about being sick?"

"It was nothing. I just thought I drank too much and I shouldn't have been driving. When I thought back, I only had a couple of beers. There's no way what I drank could have made me pass out." Colt replied.

"Maybe we should talk to a few people who were at the bar with you and Lucas that night." Detective Rogers replied.

"Do you mind if we take your cell phone and copy the recording you made? We'll return it to you as soon as we can." Detective Sloan asked as he reached for the phone.

"Sure. Take it if it will help." Cassy picked up her cell phone and handed it to Detective Sloan.

"We would like to do some investigating. Maybe talk to Mrs. Harding on our own." Both Detectives stood up from the couch and headed towards the front door.

"What do we do now?" Cassy stood up and put her arms around Colt as they walked the detectives to the front door.

"I would suggest you guys do nothing. I wouldn't talk to anyone about this, but I would suggest you take a few precautions like locking your doors during the day and at night, know where each of you are at all times." Detective Sloan replied.

"We'll wait to hear from you then." Cassy replied as they watched both detectives climb into their car and drive off. She hugged Colt as tight as she could. She was afraid for him as much as she was for herself.

18

  Dinner was quiet. Cassy noticed Colt was trying to make conversation to break the silence. Since Detectives Sloan and Rogers had left, he hadn't let her out of his site. He insisted she go with him to finish the chores on the farm. When they finished, they showered then started dinner. Cassy wasn't very hungry but she didn't want to hurt Colt's feelings. He had gone to the trouble of frying chicken, making mashed potatoes and gravy.
  "Thank you for making dinner. It's really good. Your fried chicken is much better than mine. You're going to have to teach me how to make it."
  "It's a family secret passed down from my grandmother's grandmother. I don't think I can give it to you."
  Cassy saw that cute smile on his face, the corner of his mouth turned up. She loved his smile. It put her at ease.
  "Really. Exactly what do I have to do to get the recipe?" Cassy leaned over and took his hand.

"The first thing you have to do is marry me." Colt replied. "Unless your last name is Matthews you'll never get it."

Cassy dropped her fork on the table. "Did you just ask me to marry you Colt Matthews?"

"Yes, I believe I did. What do you say?" Colt asked as he picked her up out of her chair. "You know I'm crazy about you."

"Yes, I'll marry you Colt. I love you, too." She laughed as he twirled her around the kitchen floor.

"Well, well. Isn't this a sweet moment. I'm glad I was here to share it."

Cassy and Colt stopped and turned towards the door. Lucas Harding was standing right inside the back door.

"Lucas." Cassy exclaimed. "What are you doing here?"

"I thought I would stop by and see how my half-sister and future business partner was doing. It looks like you guys are doing great. Are we celebrating something?"

"Colt just asked me to marry him." Cassy smiled at Colt trying to break the tension in the air.

"Well congratulations you two." Lucas walked in the kitchen and grabbed a piece of chicken from the platter on the table and took a bite. "This is good stuff. You're marrying a great cook Colt."

"Actually Colt fried the chicken. I'm the one marrying the great cook." Cassy smiled.

"I'm just learning all kinds of things about you two. It will come in handy when I move in the take over my share of the farm."

"What do you want Lucas?"

Cassy noticed the expression on Colt's face change. He wasn't happy with the conversation.

"And while we're at it, how did you get in the house? I locked the back door."

"I know where you keep the spare key. I had to use it a few times when old man Conner was alive. He told me where the spare key was just in case we couldn't get in the house on one of our calls. I have to give the old man his props. He was always prepared."

"Lucas, my lawyer said the results of our testing wouldn't be back for another three to four weeks. After that we still have to go through processes. It will probably be six months to a year before everything is settled legally. Aren't you jumping the gun a little bit coming out here?" Cassy took the plates off the table and carried them to the sink.

"What, you guys aren't going to finish your dinner? Don't tell me it's because of me." Lucas laughed.

Cassy could feel the chill run up her spine when he laughed like that. It was almost the same feeling she had when she visited Sarah Harding yesterday. She had to keep her cool and get him to leave. Cassy knew Colt wasn't going to be comfortable until Lucas left.

"We just finished eating right before you walked in the door. Help yourself. I'm just going to clean up."

Cassy picked up some more empty plates off the table and carried them to the sink. She noticed Lucas stand up from the table and walk into the living room. He stopped and looked around.

"So it looks like I'll get the old man's room when I move in."

"If and when that time comes, we'll discuss that. Until then, my grandfather's stuff stays right where it is." Cassy was now getting frustrated with Lucas' attitude.

"Is there some reason you're here other than to be annoying?" Cassy asked.

"Annoying? I don't think I'm being annoying. I'm just looking to the future and how things are going to work."

"You go ahead and plan all you want but I don't believe it's going to work out like you think it's going to." Cassy dried her hands on a hand towel. "You seem to think you are going to move in here and just take over. It's not going to work that way." Cassy replied. "I don't think you're even going to set foot on the Conner farm.

"You have a spitfire here Colt. I bet that's what you love about her. Does she carry that over to the bedroom?" Lucas grinned as he stuffed another piece of chicken in his mouth.

Cassy's body stiffened and her face became hot as her cheeks turned red. Lucas had succeeded in pissing her off. She wasn't going to put up with any more. Just as Cassy began to tell him exactly what she thought of his comment, she felt Colt take her by the shoulders and ground her in her place.

"Lucas, you're way out of line. You owe Cassy an apology and then I think you need to leave. You've overstayed your welcome." Colt replied. "Drop the spare key on the table before you leave."

"You think so." Lucas dropped the key in his hand on the table.

"I know so."

Cassy felt Colt push her to the side and step between Lucas and her.

"Let's go." He took Lucas by the arm and led him towards the door.

"It was good to see you again Sis. Don't worry, it won't be that long before you and I will see each other again. Maybe next time it will be just you and me and you won't have a body guard."

Cassy watched Colt push Lucas out the door towards his truck. Lucas lost his balance and almost fell. Colt didn't move. He stood frozen like a statue

"Colt." Cassy yelled. "He's not worth getting upset over. Come back in the house."

"Not until he leaves."

Cassy knew Colt wasn't going to budge until Lucas was in his truck, past the end of the driveway and out of sight. Cassy walked outside and put her arms around his waist.

"What are we going to do Colt? Lucas is going to keep it up until he owns part of the farm or lives here with us. I don't think I can handle that."

"The first thing we are going to do is change the locks on all the doors and hide the damn spare key."

****

Cassy gave up trying to sleep. She glanced at the clock and it read six am. She slipped quietly out of bed so not wake Colt. He insisted he was staying with her last night. After he had gone around the house and closed all the downstairs windows and double bolted the back and front doors. There was no way anyone could have gotten into the house during the night without waking either one of them up.

Wrapping up in her bathrobe she headed downstairs to make coffee and start something for breakfast. She walked around the house opening windows on the lower level to let the breeze blow through. It was going to heat up by early afternoon. The sooner she could cool down the house the better.

The coffee was done and Cassy was cooking some bacon on the stove. She opened a can biscuits and put them in the oven.

"It smells wonderful in here."

Cassy turned to see Colt walking down the stairs, shirtless, buttoning his jeans. He was gorgeous and every time she looked at him she realized how lucky she was and he loved her.

"I wasn't sleeping very well so I thought I would give up and come make breakfast. Would you like some eggs, bacon and biscuits?"

"That'll be great. What can I do?"

Cassy felt him come up behind her and put his arms around her waist, kissing her neck. "You can keep doing that all you want."

"That's fine with me but it won't get your breakfast eaten."

"Ok, why don't you hand me two plates then put some silverware and napkins on the table please."

"Wow, I thought maybe after last night I had earned breakfast in bed."

Cassy turned around to face him.

"You were wonderful last night. Not quite breakfast in bed material." Cassy laughed.

"Ouch, that hurt. I thought I was at the top of my game."

"I think you were still a little distracted by our visitor last night."

"You mean Lucas. Maybe you're right. I kept waking up all night making sure everything was quiet. I even got up a few times and walked around the house thinking I heard something. Lucas acted weird last night. I didn't like it at all."

"We really shouldn't be letting him or what his mother said get to us. I don't think he's stupid enough to try and take both of us out so he can inherit the ranch." Cassy took the eggs from the refrigerator and whipped them up in a bowl before emptying them into the pan.

"Your right, I know. He's surely not crazy enough to try something."

Cassy took two glasses out of the cabinet and handed them to Colt. She watched as he headed to the refrigerator to pour each of them a glass of milk. She put each of them a plate of eggs on the table and sat down in one of the empty chairs.

"So what do you have to do today around the farm?" Cassy asked as Colt sat down next to her handing her a glass of milk.

"I have lots of chores. I've been a little distracted this past week."

Colt patted Cassy's leg.

"Why don't you come help me? We can be finished before lunch then we can drive into town and have lunch at the café. We can have a delicious cheeseburger and I can see Fannie. I'll kill two birds with one stone."

"Really?" Cassy smiled. "You think so."

"I know Fannie would be happy with my performance even if it wasn't on top of my game."

Cassy laughed so hard she almost spurted milk through her nose.

"So now I'm in competition with Fannie. That's nice to know."

Cassy felt Colt take her hand in his.

"I thought we could stop at the jeweler in town and see if we can find a diamond to go on that pretty little finger of yours."

"Are you serious?"

"Very serious. How about it?"

"You have a deal." Cassy jumped up from her chair and hugged Colt's neck. "You make me very happy Colt Matthews."

"So then go get work clothes on and let's get started on the chores. How well you're on top of your game today will determine the size of rock that will go on that finger."

"So that's how it's going to be huh?"

"I thought I would give it a try. It seemed to work for you this morning."

"You're out of you league Colt Matthews. Don't even try to compete with the pro."

Cassy jumped up from Colt's lap and started up the stairs.

"I'll meet you down here after I've changed. Make sure you take care of the breakfast dishes."

"Not funny Cassy. That diamond is getting smaller and smaller."

****

Cassy was searing from the heat of the day but also from spending the morning watching a shirtless Colt take care of chores around the farm. She helped as much as she could but most of her time was spent admiring Colt and his spectacular build. He would catch her looking and laugh. Cassy knew he realized what she was doing and was putting on a show for her. She loved it.

"Are we done yet?" Cassy asked as Colt climbed back on the four-wheeler. "We've checked the fence, made sure the cattle was still grazing in the pasture you want them in, chased a few of them out of the pond. What's left?"

"If you're going to be a cattle farmer you're going to have to tough it up lady." Colt laughed.

"That's what I have you for. I'm never going to be able to keep up with you. I'm not even going to try."

"I see. I'm not only eye candy but your chore boy."

"You love it and you know it." Cassy put her arms around Colt's waist. "Take me home, have your way with me and then take me into town and buy me that diamond."

"You got it lady."

Cassy felt Colt reeve up the four-wheeler and take off. Before she knew it they were back at the house.

****

They both showered and dressed. As usual Colt was waiting downstairs for Cassy to finish dressing. When she came down the stairs, he whistled from the kitchen.

"Thanks." Cassy kissed him on the cheek. "Are you ready to go?"

"I've been ready for half an hour. I've been waiting on you." Colt laughed. "And, I must say, you are totally worth the wait."

"That's so sweet of you." Cassy snuggled up next to him. She smelled wonderful and felt almost as good.

"Are you ready to go? I'm starving and we want to have time at the jeweler before they close."

"I'm ready." Cassy grabbed his arms before he got too far away from her. "Are you sure about this Colt?"

He took her in his arms and kissed her deep and hard.

"I'm positive. I love you Cassy Conner."

"Let's go then." Colt watched Cassy run out the back door. He followed close behind.

Cassy jumped in the passenger side of Colt's truck. He opened the driver's side and climb in right behind her.

"Buckle your seat belt." Colt insisted.

"You know I hate seat belts." Cassy replied. "They wrinkle my clothes."

"I don't care if you don't like them." Colt reached across the seat and buckled Cassy's seat belt. "You're wearing it."

"You really do love me." Cassy smiled as Colt kissed her.

"Yes I do."

"I trust your driving." Cassy unhooked her seatbelt smiling at Colt.

Colt shook his head, started the engine and headed out the driveway to the road. He rolled up the windows, set the air conditioner to a comfortable temp and turned the radio up. He knew Cassy liked to sing to the radio. She had a beautiful voice. She could sing as well as some of the popular country singers he heard on the radio. Colt tried to get her to come along with him and sing at the karaoke contests they had at the bar in town. He was positive she would beat out all the other singers. One of her favorite songs came on the radio *Skinny Dipping* and she started singing along.

Colt smiled and listened trying to keep his eyes on the road and pay attention to Cassy. He noticed another truck coming atop the hill. Colt pulled over closer to the side of the road and tapped the brakes.

"Shit." Colt exclaimed.

"What's wrong?" Cassy asked.

"I don't know." Colt grabbed the steering wheel. He could feel his body tense up as he pumped the brakes. There was nothing. They pushed all the way through to the floor board. He had to keep his cool. He couldn't get Cassy upset. All he could do was try to control the truck until it slowed down. The gravel on the country road wasn't giving him much help. There was no side road to drive off. There was nothing but trees, fences and ditches along the way. Colt tried to stay out of the ditches.

"Colt, slow down." Cassy shouted.

"I'm trying Cassy. I don't have any brakes." Colt answered.

"What do you mean no brakes? You mean we can't stop?"

"I'm trying to slow down and it's not working. I need to find something to run into that won't kill us. Put your seatbelt on." Just as Colt's words left his mouth a dump truck came at them from over the next incline. Colt moved closer to the edge of the road to give him room to pass. As soon as he hit the edge, he could feel the gravel pulling them into the ditch.

"Hold on Cassy. I'm losing control."

The next thing Colt remembered was the truck rolling into the ditch and flipping over. They came to rest in a farm field. Colt was stunned. He tried to lift his head to see if he could see Cassy. He didn't hear anything coming from her side of the truck.

"Cassy. Cassy, are you all right? Colt still didn't hear anything. He tried to move his arms and unhooked his seat belt.

"Hey man. Are you all right?" Colt heard a voice coming from outside the truck,

"Don't move. We've called an ambulance and they will be here soon."

Colt could see a young man looking in the windshield of the truck.

"How's my fiancé?" Colt asked as he finally managed to move enough to be able to turn and check Cassy.

"Where is she?" Colt didn't see Cassy anywhere. The passenger door of the truck was gone and so was Cassy.

"Where the hell is she?" Colt screamed looking up at the young man. He tried to move his legs but they were stuck.

"Go find my fiancé." Colt yelled at the young man. "She was in the truck with me. Oh my god. Please, go find her."

"I'll go look. Stay calm man. The ambulance will be here in a minute. I'll go look." Colt watched as the kid disappeared into the field. It seemed forever before he came back.

"Did you find her?" Colt asked. He could tell by the look on the kids face it wasn't going to be good news.

"Yeah man. I found her. She's must have been thrown from the truck. She's still alive but she's unconscious."

Colt heard the words but didn't want them to register. He tried to move his legs again but no luck. He beat his hands against the steering wheel in frustration.

"Go stay with her until they get here, please. I'm fine. Just make sure she's all right." Colt could feel the tears running down his cheeks. "Go. Make sure she's all right."

"I will. You keep calm. I'll go stay with her and make sure the rescue people know where she is. Stay calm man. They're almost here."

Colt watched the kid disappear in the field again. He finally could hear the sirens in the distance. He just had to keep his cool until they could get to Cassy. All he could do right now was pray.

****

Colt woke to the sound of metal crunching. He looked up to see the firemen working to pry him out of the truck. He's legs were stuck underneath the steering column. Sharp pains like knives stabbing him shot through his legs with each crunch of the metal. One of the firemen was inside the cab of the truck with Colt. He had crawled through the passenger side of the truck which had lost the door and Cassy.

"How's Cassy." Colt managed to get the words out.

"Is Cassy the woman with you?"

"Yes. How is she?"

"They're checking her out now."

"Is she all right?" Colt asked waiting for answer from the fireman.

"I wish I could say for sure. They are working on her and I'm here with you. Let's get you out and then I'll go find out for you."

"Then hurry up and get me the hell out of here. I need to know if she's all right."

"We're working as hard as we can. It'll be just a few more minutes. Let's concentrate on you right now, okay?"

Colt took a deep breath. He could feel the frustration building and he had to keep it in control. He needed to get to Cassy and that's all he could think about right now.

"He's free. Let's get him out." The fireman in the cab with Colt yelled. The fireman outside the cab opened the driver's door and grabbed Colt under the arms pulling him backwards out of the cab. Colt flinched with every inch they moved him. The pain shot through each of his legs.

"As soon as we get you out I can check you better and I can give you something for the pain. Just hang in there a few more minutes man. Okay?"

Colt could only nod to the fireman in the cab with him acknowledging his request. He felt them put him on a stretcher and begin moving him out of the field. He looked around trying to find Cassy but he couldn't see her anywhere.

"Where's Cassy." Colt asked as they began to put him in the ambulance. "Where's Cassy?" He grabbed the arm of the fireman next to him.

"They've already taken her to the hospital. She'll be there when we get you there."

"How is she? Is she all right?"

"She had some nasty injuries. She was thrown from the truck. They'll know more when they get her to the hospital. Now let's get you there so we can check you out."

Colt lay back on the stretcher as a paramedic climbed in the ambulance with him. He watched the two firemen shut the doors and they drove away. All he wanted right now was Cassy. He needed to know if she was all right and he couldn't get anyone to answer him. He didn't care what was wrong with him. He needed to know about Cassy.

****

Colt wanted to climb off the table and go search the hospital for Cassy. He knew she was here but he didn't know where or how she was. No one would tell him anything. If he could make his legs cooperate, he would. He could hear the nurses and doctors talking, asking for tests to be done and for blood to be drawn. He just wanted to find Cassy.

"Mr. Matthews. I'm Dr. Williams. You're a very lucky man. You seem to be checking out all right. Just a few bumps and brushes and a broken leg."

"A broken leg?" Colt asked. "That's great. How am I going to take care of the farm with a broken leg?"

"We'll worry about that later. Right now you need to rest. We want to run some more tests and take some more x-rays."

"I need to go home and take care of the farm. When do I get out of here?" Colt asked.

"We need to keep you at least overnight. You might have to make arrangements for the farm until we can let you go."

"I want to know about Cassy Conner. Where is she? How is she?"

"Cassy had a few more injuries than you. She is in the next room being checked out by Dr. Jones. I promise as soon as Dr. Jones knows anything she'll be in here to talk to you."

"Is she all right? That's all I need to know. Is she all right?" Colt asked.

"She's stable for now. From what I can tell and what Dr. Jones has said, she hit her head pretty hard and but she is a very lucky young lady. She doesn't have any broken bones, just lots of bumps and bruises. She wasn't wearing her seat belt was she?"

"No. I tried to get her to put it on but she wouldn't. She said it wrinkled her clothes. I don't know why I didn't make her put it on." Colt replied.

"Next time you will." Dr. Williams patted him on the arm.

"You bet your ass I will." Colt replied.

19

"You have a visitor Cassy." The nurse smiled as she wheeled Colt through the hospital room door.

"Colt." Cassy whispered.

"Cassy. Are you all right?"

She felt him reach out and take her hand in his kissing it lightly.

"I have been so worried about you."

"I'm fine." Cassy answered. "You look like you've been pretty beat up."

"I feel like I've been pretty beat up. I'm going to be fine though. I got a chance to call Chad Thompson and he is going to make sure the farm is taken care of until we get out of the this place so don't worry about anything. You just concentrate on getting better." Colt replied.

Cassy smiled at Colt. He was worried about her she could tell. She could feel the love he felt for her coming through. She knew he wanted to take care of her and she loved him for that.

"What about you?" Cassy asked. "How do you plan on riding a horse, much less taking care of the cattle and running around the farm with a cast on your leg?"

"You don't know me very well do you? I can manage just about anything. You wait and see."

Cassy knew he was just trying to make her not worry about how the ranch was going to run. She was worried. Colt was always there to take care of things when her grandfather was sick. Now there wasn't anyone she knew of to help for a long period of time.

"I know you don't believe me Cassy but everything will be fine. You get better and let me worry about the farm. It's been my responsibility for a long time now. I can handle it."

Cassy knew he was serious. She felt better but was still worried. She didn't know how but she believed he could do what he said. Closing her eyes she wanted to fall back to sleep.

****

Colt sat by Cassy's bedside for a while after she fell asleep. He didn't want to leave her alone. He was afraid he would lose her. He knew he was lucky she was still here with him and he didn't want to let her out of his sight.

"Mr. Matthews." Colt turned to see Detectives Sloan and Rogers standing outside Cassy room. "May we talk to you?"

"Sure." Colt managed to turn his wheelchair around to face the two Detectives. "What can I do for you?"

"We wanted to ask you some questions about the accident. Do you feel up to answering?" Detective Sloan asked.

"I'm fine. I don't know what I can tell you but ask away."

"Can you remember what happened to make you roll your truck?"

"I just remember trying to brake to slow down because there was a truck topping the hill and there was nothing."

"What do you mean there was nothing." Detective Sloan asked.

"I mean I could put the brake pedal all the way to the floor and there was nothing. The truck wouldn't slow down at all. There were no brakes."

"So what did you do then?"

"I tried to grab the piles of gravel to give us some traction and slow us down. I looked for something to run into besides the ditch. I couldn't find anything. The next thing I knew there was a dump truck coming over the hill and I tried to move over as far as I could and I must have gone too far. I was in the ditch and we rolled." Colt rubbed his head. "I don't know how the brakes could have gone that fast. I just had the truck in for service last week and she checked out perfect."

"We don't believe this was an accident Mr. Matthews. With everything Ms. Conner told us about her grandfather, the recording she provided us and now this. We believe they may all be connected. We would like your permission to inspect your truck." Detective Sloan asked.

"Sure, whatever you need." Colt couldn't believe what he was hearing. "So you think someone did this to try and hurt us? Cassy and me?"

"We aren't sure Mr. Matthews but please, don't mention this to anyone. We need to be able to investigate without it getting out."

"Sure. I won't say a word." Colt replied.

"We would like permission to inspect Ms. Conner's truck also. We want to make sure the same thing wasn't done to her truck."

"Go ahead. Inspect whatever you need if it will prove what you want. By the way Detective Sloan, Lucas Harding was at the Conner Ranch last night. He stopped by, I believe, just to be a pest to Cassy. I watched him get in his truck and drive away. Are you thinking he had something to do with this?"

"I really don't want to say yes or no. I know we want to do some more investigating. You and Ms. Conner will be the first to know what we find out."

Colt shook Detectives Sloan and Roger's hands as they prepared to leave.

"We'll be in touch. If you think of anything that might help us, please call."

"Thank you for stopping by." Colt replied.

****

"Colt." Cassy woke up looking around the empty hospital room. Everything started coming back. She remembered the look on Colt's face as he tried to control the truck. After that, everything went blank. The next thing she remembered was waking up in the hospital emergency room.

Cassy heard someone else in the room with her but it was too dark to see. Normally the nurses turn on the light above the bed.

Feeling for the call button, she couldn't find it attached to her pillow. Cassy reached for the button on the side of the bed to turn on the lights but the rails were down. She began to panic. Her heart was beating faster and her breathing started getting shallow.

"Who's there?" Cassy asked. "I know someone is in the room. Why don't you show me who you are?"

"You were sleeping so peacefully, I didn't want to interrupt you."

Cassy recognized the voice. It was Lucas. What was he doing here in the dark? Cassy wasn't even sure what time of the day or night it was. She wasn't even sure what day it was.

"Lucas, is that you?" Cassy asked.

"Very good. I should have known you would recognize my voice even if you couldn't see me."

"What are you doing here? It's late. Why aren't you home in bed?"

"I wanted to see you...Sister."

Cassy could feel Lucas move closer to her bed.

"I was so worried about you I couldn't sleep. I just wanted to see for myself you were all right."

Cassy felt him sit down on the side of the bed. She could make out his shadow from the light shining through the door he had left open just a crack.

"I heard about your accident and I wanted to see for myself you were all right. It sounds like Colt needs to take some driving lessons. I don't know if I should let him drive you around anymore."

"We're both going to be fine."

"That's what I hear about Colt but you hit your head pretty hard. They are watching you pretty close because you have been going in and out of consciousness. You see it wouldn't be uncommon at all for someone who hit their head as hard as you did to just drift off into a coma or stop breathing all together." Lucas laughed. "I believe the stop breathing all together is the way it is going to be."

Cassy could see Lucas holding up a pillow he began putting up to her face.

"It's been nice knowing you Sister. It's too bad we didn't have more time to get to know each other better. If you would have kept you nose out of my business, it wouldn't come to this. We could have shared the farm and been a happy little family...well, at least family."

Cassy put her hands up to stop the pillow from covering her face.

"What are you talking about, your business?" Cassy asked.

"You interfered with my mother. She should have never told you my secret. I knew I couldn't trust her to keep her mouth shut. Even if she is out in space most the time she remembers everything. Now you're the only other one who knows about me giving your grandfather an extra shot of insulin. Or should I say, our grandfather. I can take care of my mother with a claim that she is crazy but don't have an explanation for you and what you know. I guess that means I have to take care of you the easy way."

Cassy could feel the pillow cover her face as she tried to push it away.

"You and Colt should have died in the crash. Well, at least you. Then I wouldn't have to do it this way. I can't keep falsifying DNA tests to prove I'm a Conner. I want that ranch and you're in my way."

The harder she tried to push the harder Lucas pushed the pillow against her face. It was getting hard to get a breath. She wanted to scream but she couldn't get enough air. She tried kicking, but her legs and feet where held tight by the bed sheets. All she could think about was Colt. This time he couldn't save her. Cassy could feel herself losing ground and then a heavy weight fell across her on the bed. Lucas' grip on the pillow loosened and she tossed it off her face and began gasping for air. She looked to see Lucas laying across her bed, out cold.

"Cassy! Are you all right?"

She couldn't believe her ears. It was Colt. She could feel him trying to drag Lucas off the top of her.

"Colt, is that you? Cassy managed to get enough air to talk.

"It's me Cassy. It's me. Just stay still."

"Lucas tried to suffocate me. He was trying to kill me. He tried to kill us."

Suddenly the lights in the room came on. Cassy could see Colt trying to balance in his wheelchair while he was tugging Lucas' leg to get him off the bed.

Two Orderlies came running in the room grabbing Lucas as he began to come to. Laying him face down on the floor they locked his hand behind his back.

"Are you all right Ms. Conner?" One of the Orderlies asked. "The nurse has paged Dr. Jones. She should be here soon."

Colt had managed to work his way up on the bed with Cassy. He held her so close she thought she was going to run out of air again.

"I'm fine Colt." She laughed. "How did you know Lucas was here?"

"I didn't. I couldn't sleep so I rolled down here to check on you. Thank goodness I did."

"Yes, thank goodness you did. He told me he gave Grandfather the shot of insulin that killed him. He told me he had to get rid of me since his mother had told me his secret. He was trying to get rid of me. He said he couldn't keep falsifying DNA tests. He's not my brother. Lucas isn't my brother."

"He was trying to kill you Cassy. Detectives Sloan and Rogers seem to think he was the reason we had the accident. They are checking out my truck to see exactly what caused me to lose my brakes."

"That's why he said we should have died in the crash. I can't believe any of this. It's like a story out of a murder mystery novel." Cassy held on to Colt as tight as she could. "Stay with me until the doctor gets here?"

"You just try to get rid of me."

Cassy and Colt watched as the two Orderlies stood Lucas up and walked him out of the room.

"Where are you taking him?" Cassy asked.

"I'm sure he's going to jail as soon as the Police arrive."

Cassy let out a sign of relief and held on to Colt.

"Does this mean we can go shopping for that diamond now?" Cassy laughed.

"Yes it does. That's exactly what it means."

20

"Good morning ladies."
Cassy turned to see Colt coming through the door way of her hospital room on crutches.
"Look at you, up and mobile."
"Dr. Williams said I could go home. What about Cassy, Dr. Jones? Can she go home with me?"
"Cassy is doing very well. Her injuries are healing well but I'd like to keep her one more night. It's nothing serious, just a precaution."
"I was hoping she could go home with me today, but if you need to keep her. I'd rather be safe than sorry." Colt made his way towards Cassy's bed and sat down on the edge.
"How about if we have that lunch I promised you before I head back to the farm? I called Fannie. She said she would make us one of her delicious cheeseburgers and have it delivered here by lunch time."
"That sounds great and it's really sweet of Fannie."
"Yes, it is. There's nothing she wouldn't do for me." Colt laughed.
"Not funny Colt." Cassy exclaimed.

"Well, I'm going to leave the two of you alone. I'll be back to check on you after lunch Cassy. Enjoy that cheeseburger."

"Thank you, Dr. Jones. I'll see you after lunch." Cassy looked at Colt disappointed. "I really wanted to go home with you today. I've missed you Colt."

"I've missed you too. It's only one more night and we'll be back at the ranch together. We won't have to worry about Lucas anymore. He's going away for a long time. We can start planning our wedding."

"I'm a very lucky lady." Cassy pulled Colt close and kissed him. She had missed that too. She would love to have him climb in bed with her but her thoughts were interrupted by someone clearing their throat.

They both turned around to see Fannie standing in the doorway.

"Sorry to interrupt you two lovebirds but I have a lunch delivery."

"Fannie, come in." Cassy smiled. "It's good to see you."

"Hi Fannie."

Cassy watched Colt stand up from the bed and kiss her on the cheek.

"It means a lot you would bring these over to us. Cassy has been craving one of your cheeseburgers for a while now."

"So you guys are both doing better, I take it?" Fannie asked.

"Yes. In fact I get to go home today. Dr. Jones wants to keep Cassy one more night. She'll be able to go home tomorrow."

"I'm glad to hear it. I have to get back to the café. Enjoy your burgers."

"Thank you again Fannie. We'll stop by and see you tomorrow before we leave."

"I'd like that. You've got a good one there Cassy. Make sure you hold on to him."

"Thank you. I plan on it." Cassy smiled as she watched Fannie walk out of the door.

"I can see I have some competition." Cassy rubbed Colt's arm.

"Not at all. There's no one who can compete with you."

Cassy hugged him tightly. She didn't want to let him go but those cheeseburgers smelled almost as wonderful as he did.

"I'm starving. How about buying a girl a cheeseburger?"

"I can do that."

Cassy moved the bed tray closer to the bed so they both could reach them. She opened the container and took a bite. "Oh my, these are wonderful."

"Yes they are. How about if we serve them at our wedding?"

"Funny."

"I hope we aren't interrupting."

"No, not at all. Please come in." Cassy replied as Detectives Sloan and Rogers walked in her hospital room door.

"May we talk to you two for a minute?"

"Yes, please sit down." Cassy adjusted herself in bed, pulling her blanket up over her.

"I'd stand up and shake your hand but it's a little difficult these days." Colt laughed.

"Don't worry Colt. You stay put. We have some news to share with the two of you."

"Is it good news?" Cassy asked.

"I'm not sure if it's necessarily good. We had your truck inspected and it looks like the brake line has been cut. So your accident wasn't really an accident. It's just as we suspected."

"Wow, so you think Lucas came back to the farm that night and cut the brake line?" Colt asked.

"Yes and since we were inspecting trucks we had them check the truck Cassy drives and also Cassy's SUV. It seems the SUV is all right but the other truck brake line was cut also. We're sure it was Lucas and we know he was trying to hurt both of you."

"That's not a big surprise especially since he tried to kill Cassy here in the hospital." Colt replied.

"Lucas Harding is in jail and the Judge refused bail so he'll be there until his trial. If we have anything to do with it, he won't get out for a long time."

"Colt and I appreciate all you two have done. You didn't have to believe me, but you did. He could have killed either one of us and gotten away with it." Cassy shuttered at the thought. Colt took her hand and held on tight.

"He's not going to touch either one of us now."

"I know, thanks to these two detectives." Cassy smiled at the two men standing at the end of her bed.

"We'll leave you alone. If you need anything or have any questions, please call us."

"We will. Thank you again."

Cassy held on to Colt as she watched the two men walk out of the room.

"I guess I need to go home and check on the farm. Are you going to be all right here without me?"

"I'm a little tired after that big cheeseburger. Can you stay with me until I fall asleep?" Cassy hugged Colt.

"That's the least I can do."

Cassy moved over to the edge of the bed so Colt could climb in next to her. Falling asleep in his arms was just what she needed.

****

"I appreciate you giving me a ride home Fannie." Colt replied. "I was trying to figure out how I was going to get them to give me a rental car with a cast on my leg."

"How are you going to get back to the hospital to pick up Cassy with that bum leg?"

"It's my right leg so I should be able to drive. Cassy's SUV is the only one left that's safe to drive and it's an automatic. I'll just drive it."

"You call me if you can't make it. The last thing we need is you having another accident."

Fannie's expression turned stern. Colt remembered that look from his mother when he was in trouble as a little boy.

"Thanks, Fannie. You're a sweetheart."

All Colt had thought about on the way back to the farm was Cassy and how much he wanted her here with him. He understood she needed to stay another night in the hospital, but it didn't make it any easier she was gone. Maybe he would sleep in his old bed in the bunkhouse tonight and he wouldn't miss her so much. "Like that's going to help."

He knew there were a lot of chores that needed to be done around the farm. He had plenty to keep him busy until she returned. As they pulled up the driveway of the farm Colt noticed another SUV with Texas plates parked next to Cassy's.

"Who the heck?" Colt exclaimed.

"Looks like you have some company." Fanny pulled up closer to the house. "You want me to stick around to make sure everything is all right?"

"I'll be fine Fannie. Thanks for looking out for me."

"You know you can't run very far or fast. Just make sure you get a good hit in with the crutches. That'll teach them a lesson." Fannie laughed.

"Kinda like what I did to Lucas Harding?"

"Yeah, something like that. Heck I have to help you out of the truck so I'll just stick around a few minutes and make sure everything's good."

Colt laughed as he watched Fannie come around to the passenger side of the truck and help him swing his cast out the door. He got his footing on the gravel driveway and headed towards the house on crutches. As he got closer to the SUV he noticed two women sitting inside.

"Can I help you?" Colt yelled as he came closer to the SUV.

"I hope so." Both women came bouncing out of the SUV barely touching the ground. "We're looking for the Conner farm. We are here to see Cassy Conner."

"You've got the right place, but Cassy's not here right now. Is there something you wanted to see her about? It looks like you drove quite a distance." Colt pointed one of his crutches at the license plate on their car.

"I guess we should introduce ourselves." The little petite blonde replied. "I'm Laura and this is Nancy. We are good friends of Cassy's from Texas. She said we should visit and since we didn't make it here for her grandfather's funeral we thought we would surprise her and show up for a few days."

"Sure, Cassy has mentioned the two of you a lot since she has come back. I'm Colt Matthews."

He put his hand out just far enough not to lose his balance on his crutches.

"Colt Matthews. So you're the farmhand Cassy's grandfather left half the ranch to." Laura reached out and shook Colt's hand. "It's a pleasure to meet you."

"Me too." Nancy reached over and shook Colt's hand. "So where is Cassy?"

"I'm afraid Cassy is in the hospital." Colt couldn't get the rest of the explanation out before both of the women were on the verge of tears hugging each other.

"Oh my, what happened?" Laura finally composed herself enough to ask.

"I tell you ladies what. It's getting a little tiring to stand on these crutches so how about if we go in the house, I'll get you both something to drink, you can freshen up and I'll tell you the whole story." Colt started walking towards the house.

"That sounds great. We'll just get our suitcases and join you in the house."

"Suitcases?" Colt looked at Fannie.

"You're on your own with this one Stud. I'm leaving." Fannie put her hands up in the air and headed back to her truck. "Make sure you stop in the café and tell me all about your evening when you come to pick Cassy up tomorrow."

Colt watched Fannie laughing all the way to her truck.

"Thanks Fannie. I thought you were a friend." Colt saw her wave as she backed out of the driveway and headed back into town. He was sure she got a good laugh at his expense. He hobbled into the kitchen and took the picture of tea out of the refrigerator then grabbed two glasses from the cabinet and sat them down at the table.

"Iced tea isn't going to cut it." Colt hobbled back to the refrigerator and pulled out a beer and sat down at the table just in time for Laura and Nancy to walk in the back door both dragging a huge suitcase and tote bag. Colt could only hope they weren't planning to stay the rest of the summer.

"So where will we be staying?" Laura asked.

"Well Cassy's room is at the top of the stairs on the right. There's a guest bedroom if you guys want to share next door to that one. There's also a bathroom on that floor. I would say you could stay in Cassy's grandfather room but he died in there."

"Eww! That's all right. We'll share the guest bedroom upstairs." Nancy replied.

"So where do you sleep Colt?"

Colt could swear he saw Laura wink at him as she sat down at the table and poured her and Nancy a glass of iced tea.

"I sleep in the bunkhouse out past the barn."

"So you'll be around to protect us in case we get scared right?" Laura smiled.

"Sure." Colt took a sip of beer thinking how this could be a disaster.

"So tell us how Cassy ended up in the hospital."

"We had a car accident." Colt started to explain.

"Oh how awful." Laura interrupted. "Was it scary?"

"It was really scary." Colt rolled his eyes at the thought of how he was worried about being bored tonight. "We lost our brakes when we were going into town and I rolled the truck. Cassy was thrown out because she wasn't wearing her seatbelt. My leg was broken but we are both lucky to be alive."

"That's sounds horrible. Poor Cassy. So it's a good thing we're here." Laura nodded at Nancy. "We can help you guys out while you recuperate. It'll be fun taking care of you and Cassy. So can we go with you tomorrow to bring her home? We can surprise her."

"Oh I'm sure you'll surprise her. She has no clue you guys are here."

"Please don't tell her Colt." Nancy pleaded. "It will be fun to see the look on her face when we show up tomorrow at the hospital."

"So are you ladies hungry? I wasn't planning on fixin' much for dinner but we can see what there is for sandwiches or I know there's some fried chicken we can have."

"How about if we order a pizza and have it delivered or grab some fast food? That way we don't have to cook."

Colt almost choked on his beer when he couldn't help but laugh.

"I'm sorry ladies but you are in the middle of nowhere Oklahoma. We don't have pizza delivery or any fast food restaurants close enough to grab. The closest restaurant we have is the City Café and its several miles down the road in town. I'll show it to you tomorrow when we go into town to pick up Cassy."

"It's going to be a long week."

Colt saw a sigh come from Nancy's lips as she looked at Laura.

"Week?" Colt asked.

"We were planning to stay a week if you guys can stand us that long. Besides it looks like the two of you are going to need help that long. Maybe we can help you around the farm feeding the chicken, cows, horses or whatever it is you have on the farm."

"That should be fun. I'll keep it in mind. Let's check out dinner and then we can get you guys settled in."

****

Colt managed to find something to satisfy everyone's dinner tastes. He watched as Nancy and Laura cleaned up the kitchen and put everything back where it belonged. Cassy would be proud of them. Colt was sure it was going to take more directions but they both seemed to be able to handle the mess. Maybe a week wasn't going to be as long as he thought. They could handle helping around the house. He knew Cassy wasn't going to be up to cleaning and cooking when she came home tomorrow and he certainly couldn't do much with his leg in a cast.

"So, Colt, why don't you tell us about you and Cassy." Nancy sat down at the table next to him.

"What do you mean?" Colt could tell his face was going to give him away.

"Are the two of you dating, sleeping together, in love, friends with benefits, what?"

"I think I'll leave that for Cassy to answer for you tomorrow. I'm sure you girls will have a good time catching up on everything that's been going on here lately."

"Really, like what?"

"I'm not going to spoil Cassy's fun so ladies, I think I am going to turn in for the night."

Colt stood up, grabbing his crutches and headed for the backdoor. "Make sure you lock up. I've got a key. I'll see you tomorrow morning bright and early. Good night."

Making his way across the driveway Colt opened the door to the bunkhouse. Walking through the door he tossed his crutches down on the floor and headed for the bedroom. He already missed Cassy. He was ready for her to come home tomorrow even if it meant her girlfriends were sticking around for a week.

21

"Well at least they listened to me about locking the doors." Colt balanced himself on his crutches and pulled his key out of his pocket to let himself in the house. No one was awake. It had taken him a little longer to get around this morning because he had to figure out how to climb in and out of the bathtub with the cast on his leg. If Cassy would have been there she would have been able to help. As much as he missed her he was afraid they wouldn't have gotten much farther than the bedroom.

He decided to make some coffee and start breakfast before Laura and Nancy woke up. He started bacon in a pan on the stove and then ran the water for the coffee pot. He took the bread out of the breadbox and put a few slices in the toaster.

"It smells good in here."

Colt turned to see Laura standing in the doorway minus a few pieces of clothing. He turned back to what he was doing trying not to notice how little she was wearing.

"What do ya'll like for breakfast? Can I make you some eggs? Colt asked.

"I normally don't eat much for breakfast. I usually grab something when I get to work."

"We talked about that grabbin' something thing last night. It ain't happenin'." Colt laughed.

"Oh right. So do you have any cereal and fruit?" Laura asked.

"That sounds good." Nancy added as she walked through the kitchen door. "Or maybe a bagel."

Colt turned around and leaned against the kitchen cabinet crossing his arms and feeling the frustration building in the pit of his stomach.

"Ok ladies. Let's get this straight. I'm making bacon, eggs and toast for breakfast. If you want cereal there may be some in the pantry, you'll have to look. There are some strawberries in the fridge and some peaches in the bowl on the table. Forget the bagel. So what's it going to be?" Colt waited for a minute and got no reply. Throwing his hand up in the air, he turned back to his bacon cooking on the stove.

"Ok, so you're on your own. One more thing, I'll be leaving for the hospital in one hour so if you want to go with me, be ready."

"Gees."

Colt could feel the daggers piercing his back.

"I'll take two eggs over-easy and a piece of dry toast." Laura replied.

"Me too." Nancy piped in after her.

"You got it ladies. There is just one more thing."

"What now?" Laura squealed.

"Go put some clothes on or you're not eating at the same table with me."

Colt kept cooking and never turned around. He knew if he did he would lose control laughing. These two were the easiest fish he had ever reeled in. Opposites must attract because there is no way Cassy was ever like the two of them. If she acted like the two of them when they were together, Colt was sure he couldn't take it.

"Just shoot me now."

****

With his and Cassy pickup's in the shop being repaired, Colt's only option was to drive Cassy's SUV. It was probably a good idea anyway because Laura and Nancy were tagging along with him. That is if they ever finished dressing they were tagging along.

Getting anxious Colt honked the horn hoping to get results. Nothing.

"Ladies, this taxi leaves in five minutes." Colt yelled out the window. Reaching down he turned on the radio and *Skinny Dipping* was on. "I hope this isn't a sign."

"We're ready to go."

Colt watched Nancy climb in the passenger seat of the SUV.

"Laura's right behind me."

"It's about time. Do you ladies always take this long to get around?" Colt laughed.

"We hurried, if you must know." Laura snipped as she climbed in the back seat tossing a bag in the back. "I went easy on the makeup and didn't do much with my hair. I hope Cassy doesn't mind us showing up like this."

"I feel sorry for whoever marries you guys. He's going to be spending half his time waiting on you to get ready."

"Maybe, but look at the two of us, we're worth the wait."

Colt caught a glimpse of Laura posing in the back seat.

"All I know is Cassy can get around in less than five minutes and look beautiful. I don't think I've ever seen her take more than thirty minutes. You guys take forever."

"Can we change the subject please?" Nancy snapped. "I can tell right now I'm going to have to play peacekeeper between you two. I hope you can behave when we get around Cassy. She doesn't need to come home to the two of you bickering."

"How about if we call a truce Laura?" Colt asked.

"Well, all right."

Colt shook Laura's hand she extended as a peace offering.

"Great, now let's go pick up Cassy. I can't wait to see her. It's been a long time."

"That sounds like love to me." Laura giggled.

"She'll be happy to see both of you. I'm sure there is not a bigger surprise I could give her. Now, buckle up and let's go."

Colt headed out the driveway and into town. The ride was completely quiet all the way.

****

Pulling into the parking lot of the hospital, Colt opened the door and climbed out grabbing his crutches from between the seats.

"Let's go ladies." Colt shut the door and waited for the two of them to straighten their hair in the rearview mirror; both of them put on fresh lipstick, and then climb out of the SUV straightening their clothes.

"Lord, help me. These two primp enough for the rest of the world."

He locked the doors of the SUV and headed towards the hospital doors.

"Colt, wait up." Nancy asked.

"Yeah, we need to get Cassy's suitcase out of the back. Unlock the doors."

Colt reached in his pocket and pushed the button on the key. He watched as Laura opened the hatch door and pulled out a small suitcase. He was so anxious to see Cassy he had forgotten to bring her anything to wear home from the hospital. The clothes she was brought in wearing had to be thrown out. They were covered with blood and stains.

"Thank you for remembering to pack her some clean clothes. I completely forgot." Colt replied.

"What do you think we were doing all the time you thought we were primping? Gawd, you think we were only putting on makeup and fixing our hair?"

"Well, I guess you put me in my place. I'm sorry. Now can we go get Cassy?"

"Let's go." Laura took one of Colt's arms and Nancy took the other as he hobbled in the hospital door on crutches.

"You're not so bad after all." Laura winked.

"Her rooms right down here." Colt pointed down the hallway.

"You go in first. We want to surprise her." Laura said. "If that's all right with you, Colt?"

"It's perfectly fine with me. Hang on to the suitcase and I'll let you know when to come in." Colt peeked inside the door smiling at the sight of Cassy sleeping. He quietly walked to the edge of the bed and kissed her lightly on the cheek. "Hi Gorgeous."

"Colt." Cassy sat up in the bed and hugged his neck as tight as she could. "I've missed you so much."

"I missed you too." Colt sat down on the bed. "Has Dr. Jones said you can go home yet?"

"She's supposed to be in any minute now. I'm so ready to go home. I can't stand being in this hospital room without you." Cassy looked around the room. "Wait a minute. Colt did you forget to bring me something to wear home?"

"Well."

"Colt, I don't see a suitcase or even an overnight bag. You forgot didn't you?"

"Yes, I did forget."

"Colt, you didn't." Cassy replied.

"But...I had some help remembering and they also came with me to carry it in. Ladies, come on in."

"Oh my goodness. Laura. Nancy. What are you guys doing here?" Cassy squealed.

"We've missed you and we were so sorry we didn't make it for your grandfather's funeral so we decided to surprise you and come for a visit."

"Come give me a hug?" Cassy held her arms out and they both rushed towards her.

"It is so good to see you both. I can't believe you're here. When did you get here?"

"We got here yesterday afternoon." Laura replied.

"Where did you stay last night?" Cassy asked.

"Colt was kind enough to let us sleep in the guest bedroom of your farm."

"He did?" Cassy looked at Colt. He was smiling that crooked little smile she loved so much. "How sweet of him and just where did you sleep? May I ask?"

"I slept in my bed in the bunkhouse. Where else would I have slept?" Colt shrugged his shoulders.

"What is it with the two of you? We tried to get it out of Colt last night and he said you would fill us in on everything even why and how you ended up in the hospital. Start talking girl." Laura said.

"There's so much to tell." Cassy was interrupted by Dr. Jones walking through the door.

"Dr. Jones."

"Cassy. How are you feeling?"

"I'm feeling great. Can I go home?"

"Well, let me check you out and we'll see. It looks like you are having a party in here." Dr. Jones replied.

"Dr. Jones these are my friends from Texas, Laura and Nancy. They came to see me but they had no idea I was in the hospital."

"Well you have an interesting story to tell them don't you? If the rest of you will excuse us I'd like to check Cassy over. If she wants to go home she better have some good results."

"We'll wait outside in the hallway."

Cassy watched Laura take Nancy by the arm and walk out the door.

"Colt, are you coming?"

"I'd like him to stay ladies." Dr. Jones said as she started checking Cassy's pulse and blood pressure.

"If I let her go home today I want you to promise me you won't let her do too much. She needs to rest and not do anything to overexert herself at all. Do I make myself clear?"

"What about sex?" Colt asked.

"Colt." Cassy exclaimed.

"It's a perfectly legitimate question, Cassy. I would rather you wait a few days to make sure you are completely back to normal. It's not uncommon for people to pass out during sex with a head injury. I just want you to know the side effects."

"I promise I'll take care of her Dr. Jones. Besides with Laura and Nancy hanging around it's not like there's going to be much happening anyway."

"Can we change the subject please?" Cassy laughed.

"You can go home. You are doing great. I'll sign your paperwork and I'll expect to see you in my office next week. Call and make an appointment sometime in the next few days."

"Thank you, Dr. Jones." Cassy watched as she walked out the door and Laura and Nancy walked back in, climbing up on her bed.

"Okay, while you change, tell us all about you and Colt and how you ended up in this place." Laura asked.

"Excuse me ladies but I'm going to go get a cup of coffee and see if there is anything I can do to hurry up the paperwork." Colt kissed Cassy and headed out the door.

"That guy loves you like crazy." Nancy said.

"I know." Cassy replied. "I'm a very lucky lady."

****

They walked out of the hospital doors and Cassy looked around for Colt's truck. She remembered it was in the shop being repaired.

"Colt what car did you drive to pick me up?" She asked.

"I drove your SUV. It's the only automobile that works at the farm."

"Did you check out the license plate before you drove off?" Cassy laughed.

"No, but what about it is so funny." Colt asked.

Cassy pointed to the license plate frame she had put on her car the first day she arrived at the farm *Cowboy Butts Drive Me Nuts!*

"You mean to tell me I've been driving around town with that thing on the back of the car?"

"Yes, you have. But that one is mine. I'll have to get you one of your own for Christmas."

"Very funny. Where's a screwdriver?"

"Oh, leave it." Cassy laughed. "You won't be driving my car for long. Your truck will be fixed before you know it."

"What about my manhood? That won't be fixed for a long time. I can't have any of my friends see me driving with that on the back of my car."

"Then I'll drive. Hand over the keys so your manhood will stay in tack."

"You're not driving with your injuries. I'll just have to chance it."

Cassy, Nancy and Laura stood back and watched Colt put Cassy's tote bag and his crutches in the back of the car. Looking at each other they smiled and all three whistled.

"What the heck?"

The look on Colt's face was priceless as all three women couldn't help but laugh.

"It's those Cowboy butts." Cassy exclaimed. "They drive us nuts."

"Not funny ladies. Get in the car and let's go home. Otherwise I'm leaving you here."

Cassy climbed in the passenger side as Nancy and Laura climb in the back seat. She waited for Colt to slide in the driver's seat then she patted him on the arm.

"It's going to be a long week." Colt put his hand on hers.

"You'll love it. We can all have breakfast, lunch and dinner together; work around the farm and help you out on anything you need us to. Twenty four hours for the next seven days. You'll love it."

"Just shoot me now."

Cassy watched Colt sink down in his seat as she couldn't help but laughed.

"Just remember I love you." Cassy replied as he backed out of the hospital parking lot. "How about if we stop and get something to eat at the City Café before we head back to the ranch? Are ya'll hungry?" Cassy asked Nancy and Laura in the backseat.

"Sure. Colt told us about the café here in town. We would love to try it."

"Ok. We'll stop there first. You guys are going to love Fannie and she is going to love you too." Cassy laughed.

"Oh, they've already met. It will be a treat for her to see them again." Colt rolled his eyes.

"Okay ladies. This is the City Café." Colt pointed towards the building in front of them. "Why don't you ladies go ahead and order. Cassy and I will join you in a few minutes. We have an errand we need to run."

"What's this about?" Laura asked. "You're dumping us at the City Café."

"We're not dumping you." Colt explained. "We'll be right there. You guys entertain yourselves for a few minutes and we'll be right back." Colt waited until they both were out of the car and heading for the café. "Okay, let's go." Colt climbed out of the car and hobbled to the back to get his crutches.

"Where are we going?" Cassy asked.

"Come on. I'll show you." Colt motioned for Cassy to follow. He led her down the street a few blocks until they came to the local jewelry store. "Here we are." Opening the door while balancing on his crutches, Colt waited for Cassy to walk through the door. "Let's find a diamond for that finger."

"Colt, are you sure?"

"I've never been surer of anything in my life." Colt pulled Cassy to him and kissed her. "I love you Cassy Conner. Will you marry me?"

"Yes, I will. I love you too, Colt Matthews."

Cassy began looking through the display cases trying to find what she thought would be the perfect ring. She felt Colt watching her as she looked along with him to see if there was any type of sign she might see something she liked.

"Are you two finding anything you would like to look at?" The clerk asked.

"You have so many." Cassy replied.

"I would guess you two are looking for an engagement ring."

"You would be correct." Colt answered. "We want to see something you can't miss from a block away."

"Maybe not that big." Cassy laughed.

"So for a half a block away."

"I think I have the perfect rings. Follow me." The clerk led them around the corner of the display case as she pulled out a tray of diamond solitaires. "These are our most popular styles. Whether you want white gold, platinum or yellow gold would be the only decision."

The two carat princess cut diamond caught both their eye.

"I like that one." Colt pointed to the ring in the case.

"I was just thinking the same thing." Cassy smiled.

"Here, let's try it on." The clerk handed the ring to Cassy and watched her put in on her finger. "It's lovely."

"Yes it is." Cassy held her hand up moving it side to side watching the sun catch glimpses in the diamond. "It's beautiful."

"We'll take this one." Colt kissed her on the hand. "It's perfect."

"It looks like it fits perfectly also." The clerk replied.

"Yes it fits perfectly. Like it's meant to be mine."

"Then it's yours. Wrap it up." Colt handed the clerk his card.

"Are you sure you want me to wrap it or do you want to wear it?" The clerk asked Cassy smiling."

Cassy smiled at Colt not saying a word. She didn't have to her eyes said it all.

"She'll wear it." Colt smiled.

Heading back down the street to the café, Cassy couldn't keep her eyes off the ring. It was absolutely beautiful.

"It's about time." Laura ran up and met them as they walked through the door. "Where have the two of you been?"

Cassy didn't say a word she just held up her hand.

"What?" Nancy came bouncing up behind Laura. "Does this mean?"

"Yes. Colt and I are getting married." Cassy could feel her heart beating fast at the thought of marriage, but she wasn't afraid. Colt was her rock.

"What's this I hear? You're gettin' hitched." Fannie walked up behind Colt. "I thought you and I were goin' to get hitched someday."

"Fannie, I'm sorry you had to find out this way." Colt smiled and put his arm around her.

"I'm heartbroken." Fannie laughed. "Congratulations, you two. You make a perfect couple. Now how about something to eat? It's on me."

"Thanks Fannie. I just spent my life savings on a ring."

"Colt." Cassy hit him lightly on the arm.

"I'm kidding. Let's go sit down and order before she changes her mind."

"I already know what I want, one of your fantastic cheeseburgers." Cassy replied.

"Make that two." Colt smiled.

"You got it. Have a seat and I'll bring 'em out to you along with a pop and a beer."

"Thanks Fannie." Colt took Cassy by the hand and headed for the booth where Laura and Nancy had been sitting.

"So when are you guys planning to getting married?" Nancy asked.

"We haven't thought that far ahead." Cassy answered.

"We are coming back for the ceremony so make sure we get an invitation." Laura suggested. "It's not every day you get to attend a wedding where there is going to be a room full of cowboys dressed up in their skin tight wranglers. Wow, imagine all the cowboy butts in that room." Laura and Nancy laughed. "We're for sure coming back for that."

"Would you guys be my maid of honor and bridesmaid?" Cassy asked.

"We would love to. That would be so much fun." Laura giggled.

"We would love to." Nancy smiled.

"Great. We'll find you some good looking cowboys to walk down the aisle with. It will be great." Cassy looked at Colt smiling her 'you'll help me' smile.

"Yeah, it will be great." Colt whispered under his breath.

"What?" Cassy asked. "Did you say something?"

"No. I didn't say anything. I was just thinking how lucky my friends are going to be." Colt put his arms around Cassy. "Almost as lucky as I am."

22

"It's going to be a beautiful day Cassy."

"Yes it is." Cassy smiled as Laura and Nancy walked up behind her. "I can't believe I'm getting married today."

"I can't believe you are the first of us getting married." Laura smiled.

"Why?" Cassy asked.

"For some reason I always thought Nancy would be the first to walk down the aisle. She was always the one to have a steady boyfriend or could find a boyfriend whenever she wanted to."

"Well, you're wrong Laura." Nancy replied. "Cassy is surely beating me down the aisle but maybe not for long."

"What do you mean Nancy?" Laura asked.

"Yeah, exactly what do you mean? Are you keeping a secret from us?" Cassy moved closer to Nancy so she could hear what she had to say.

"Chad and I have gotten pretty close."

"You mean Colt's friend Chad Thompson?"

"Yes. We kept in touch after we met the last time I was here."

"I noticed you guys were getting pretty friendly at the Engagement Party we threw for Cassy and Colt." Laura replied.

"Now that you mention it, you two were gone for a little while during the party." Cassy continued. "It's all making sense. You two snuck out to be alone for a while."

"You weren't supposed to know. We didn't want to take any of the attention off of you and Colt."

"So is it serious?" Laura asked. "Why didn't you ever mention it to me after we got home?"

"Because Chad wants me to move in with him on his farm. He loves me and I love him."

"Congratulations Nancy." Laura hugged her. "That's great. I know you'll be happy. So you told him he could move in with you right?"

"No. He has a farm Laura. He can't just pick up and move. Besides, I couldn't ask him to sell his farm for me. I can move my job anywhere."

"You mean you are actually going to give up your customers to move here and start all over?"

"I don't have to give up my customers. My web design business can be done from anywhere. If I have to travel back to Texas every now and then, I can write it off as a business expense." Nancy replied.

"Wow, you have really thought this through haven't you?" Laura looked surprised.

"Chad and I have discussed it a lot over the last few months. I wanted to tell you guys so many times but I wanted Cassy to be the center of attention so I was hoping to wait until after the wedding."

"That's so sweet of you Nancy but we want to know everything good that happens to you. We want to share your happiness as much as our own." Cassy hugged her tightly. "I'm happy for you."

"Thanks Cassy." Nancy turned towards Laura. "I also didn't want to leave you alone in Texas. I was afraid if I moved here with Cassy you would be upset and alone."

"I'm a grown girl." Laura laughed. "I can take care of myself."

"I know you can. It's just I would miss you." Nancy started to tear up.

"I'd miss you too." Laura hugged the two of them. "I might just have to find me a cowboy and move here with the two of you. Right now we have a wedding to go to."

Everything was beautiful. Cassy was glad she let Colt talk her into an outdoor wedding. There was a perfect spot in the yard to set up tents for the reception and arrange seating for the ceremony. An archway of fresh white roses and matching arrangements waited at the end of the walkway of white carpet which had been placed on the ground for the wedding party to follow. Cassy couldn't have been more pleased with the way the decorations had turned out. She managed to find her wedding dress and the bridesmaid's dresses at a local shop.

"Are you ready to get married?"

Cassy turned to see Colt standing behind her.

"What are you doing here? You know it's bad luck for the groom to see the bride on their wedding day."

"You don't believe that bullshit do you?"

"I don't know. I've never been married before but that's what I've always heard." Cassy answered as Colt moved closer to her. He was so handsome in his tuxedo. She had told him he didn't need to wear a tux. She thought a nice suit would do but she was glad now. He was gorgeous.

"You look beautiful."

"Thank you." Cassy sighed. "You look very handsome."

"Thanks." Colt laughed. "If you're not doing anything for the rest of your life how about we get married?"

"I would love to. Ahh. What was your name again?"

"Colt. Colt Matthews was my name and will be yours before long."

"Cassy Matthews. Hum, that has a nice ring to it. I think I can get used to it."

"What about Mrs. Colt Matthews? That has an even nicer ring."

"Yes it does but." Cassy paused.

"But what?"

"Can I keep my first name? Both of us named Colt might be a little confusing."

"Very funny." Colt replied. "You know what I meant."

"Sure. What if we get married now?" Cassy hugged him tightly.

"Would you two break it up? Colt they are ready for you." Chad pointed towards the crowd of people.

Cassy watched him head out the door with his best man Chad. Before he reached the doorway he turned back around and smiled that smile.

"I'll be waiting for you at the end of the aisle."

Cassy could feel her heart warm. "I'll be there."

****

Cassy listened as the music played and signaled her down the aisle. Taking a deep breath, she started walking along the white walkway which had been laid on top of the grass. She felt as if her life was just beginning. This was the happiest day of her life even though tears formed in her eyes as she walked to a row of empty chairs decorated with white ribbon and bows. They were lovingly placed there in memory of her Grandmother and Grandfather Conner, her parents, Colt's Grandparents and parents. Colt joined her at the row of chairs as each of them took turns placing a white rose on the chairs. Cassy tried not to stare but she could swear there were tears in Colts eyes also. Taking her arm Colt walked with her the rest of the way down the aisle, her best friends walking right in front of her.

Colt Matthews was the answer to all of her prayers when she was a little girl. She loved him more than she could even imagine and he loved her too. Life was beautiful and the ceremony was going to be also.

"You were worth waiting for."

Cassy smiled as Colt took her hand when they reached the end of the aisle.

"I have to be the luckiest man in the world."

Cassy was lost in his eyes. She could hear the words the preacher was saying and the buzz of all the voices coming from the guests but she could only concentrate on Colt. This was a moment she would remember the rest of her life. It was the moment her mother tried to describe to her when she was a little girl. She never could understand or picture what her mother was talking about until now. There was no way anyone could describe the feelings rushing through her body at this moment. The thrill of knowing the man she loved with all her heart and soul was feeling the same feelings for her as she was for him. She was complete and whole. She wanted to let everyone she loved share this moment with them.

BIOGRAPHY

C. DEANNE ROWE

     A well written romance with a heart wrenching plot, a song with lyrics which touch your soul; nothing is more powerful. The only way would be if you were on a warm sunny beach with white sand and blue water as far as you could see. I have always loved the power of words. How they could make me cry, laugh, or provoke all range of emotions. I wouldn't be who I am without words. I learned happiness listening to songs which filled my heart. I learned the meaning of love watching all the good romance movies. Of course, there was sex which lay between the pages of the paperbacks I hid from my parents. Words have always been my friend, my comfort, my teacher. It was only logical I would grow up and want to be an author, to spin a tale which would captivate readers. My life journey has taken me in this direction and I can only hope I don't disappoint those who choose to follow.

More books in the Cowboy Temptation Series will be coming soon.

Other titles available by C. Deanne Rowe writing as Writers of the Lake:

Available on my website:
www.cdeannerowe.com

You may contact me at:
cdeanne@cdeannerowe.com

CPSIA information can be obtained at www.ICGtesting.com
Printed in the USA
LVOW102325280113

317575LV00022B/796/P